THE

ONCE

UPON A TIME IN

BATH

NY TIMES BESTSELLING AUTHOR
CHERYL BOLEN

Some of the praise for Cheryl Bolen's writing:

"One of the best authors in the Regency romance field today." – *Huntress Reviews*

"Bolen's writing has a certain elegance that lends itself to the era and creates the perfect atmosphere for her enchanting romances." – *RT Book Reviews*

The Counterfeit Countess (Brazen Brides, Book 1)
Daphne du Maurier award finalist for Best Historical Mystery

"This story is full of romance and suspense. . . No one can resist a novel written by Cheryl Bolen. Her writing talents charm all readers. Highly recommended reading! 5 stars!" – *Huntress Reviews*

"Bolen pens a sparkling tale, and readers will adore her feisty heroine, the arrogant, honorable Warwick and a wonderful cast of supporting characters." – *RT Book Reviews*

A Duke Deceived
"*A Duke Deceived* is a gem. If you're a Georgette Heyer fan, if you enjoy the Regency period, if you like a genuinely sensuous love story, pick up this first novel by Cheryl Bolen." – *Happily Ever After*

Lady By Chance (House of Haverstock, Book 1)
Cheryl Bolen has done it again with another sparkling Regency romance. . .Highly recommended – *Happily Ever After*

The Bride Wore Blue (Brides of Bath, Book 1)
Cheryl Bolen returns to the Regency England she knows so well. . .If you love a steamy Regency with a fast pace, be sure to pick up *The Bride Wore Blue*. – *Happily Ever After*

With His Ring (Brides of Bath, Book 2)
"Cheryl Bolen does it again! There is laughter, and the interaction of the characters pulls you right into the book. I look forward to the next in this series." – *RT Book Reviews*

The Bride's Secret (Brides of Bath, Book 3)
(originally titled *A Fallen Woman*)
"What we all want from a love story...Don't miss it!"
– *In Print*

To Take This Lord (Brides of Bath, Book 4)
(originally titled *An Improper Proposal*)
"Bolen does a wonderful job building simmering sexual tension between her opinionated, outspoken heroine and deliciously tortured, conflicted hero." – *Booklist of the American Library Association*

My Lord Wicked
Winner, International Digital Award for Best Historical Novel of 2011.

With His Lady's Assistance (Regent Mysteries, Book 1)
"A delightful Regency romance with a clever and personable heroine matched with a humble, but intelligent hero. The mystery is nicely done, the romance is enchanting and the secondary characters are enjoyable." – *RT Book Reviews*

Finalist for International Digital Award for Best Historical Novel of 2011.

One Golden Ring
"One *Golden Ring*...has got to be the most PERFECT Regency Romance I've read this year." – *Huntress Reviews*

Holt Medallion winner for Best Historical, 2006

Books by Cheryl Bolen
Regency Romance
Brazen Brides Series
 Counterfeit Countess (Book 1)
 The Wedding Bargain (Book 2)
 Oh What A (Wedding) Night (Book 3)
 Marriage of Inconvenience (Book 4)

House of Haverstock Series
 Lady by Chance (Book 1)
 Duchess by Mistake (Book 2)
 Countess by Coincidence (Book 3)

The Brides of Bath Series:
 The Bride Wore Blue (Book 1)
 With His Ring (Book 2)
 The Bride's Secret (Book 3)
 To Take This Lord (Book 4)
 Love in the Library (Book 5)
 A Christmas in Bath (Book 6)
 Once Upon a Time in Bath (Book 7)

The Regent Mysteries Series:
 With His Lady's Assistance (Book 1)
 A Most Discreet Inquiry (Book 2)
 The Theft Before Christmas (Book 3)
 An Egyptian Affair (Book 4)

Pride and Prejudice Sequels
 Miss Darcy's New Companion (Book 1)
 Miss Darcy's Secret Love (Book 2)
 The Liberation of Miss de Bourgh (Book 3)

The Earl's Bargain
My Lord Wicked
His Lordship's Vow
A Duke Deceived

Novellas:
Christmas Brides (3 Regency Novellas)

Inspirational Regency Romance
Marriage of Inconvenience

Romantic Suspense
Texas Heroines in Peril Series:
Protecting Britannia
Capitol Offense
A Cry in the Night
Murder at Veranda House

Falling for Frederick

American Historical Romance
A Summer to Remember (3 American Historical Romances)

World War II Romance
It Had to be You

Once Upon a Time in Bath

(The Brides of Bath, Book 7

Cheryl Bolen

Copyright © 2020 by Cheryl Bolen

Once Upon A Time in Bath is a work of fiction. Names, characters, places, and incidents are the products of the author's imagination or are used fictitiously. Any resemblance to actual events, locales, or persons, living or dead, is entirely coincidental.

All rights reserved.

No part of this publication may be reproduced, stored or transmitted in any form or by any means without the prior written permission of the author.

Prologue

Ellie Macintosh was apprehensive about meeting with Henry Wolf today. A nastier piece of work had never darkened the door of Mrs. Starr's gambling establishment, where Ellie had served as a hostess for the past three years.

When Mr. Wolf had first approached Ellie about meeting with him after work the previous night, she had most persistently turned him down. She still vividly recalled the bruises on poor, foolish Sally Smythe when that unfortunate hostess had the misfortune of *meeting* the wicked man after work one night.

Besides, Ellie wasn't that kind of girl. She dealt the *Vingt-et-Un* pasteboards night after night, but she never mingled with the patrons outside of Mrs. Starr's. And of all the men who frequented the gaming parlor, none was more repugnant to her than Henry Wolf.

One seeing him for the first time would admire the well-dressed man who was possessed of large physique and even larger fortune. It wasn't until one came face to face with him that one realized something was off.

It wasn't his extraordinarily white skin contrasting with his raven-black hair that struck a discordant note. Nor was it his pale green almost translucent eyes. She could not articulate why this man with an outwardly inoffensive appearance brought to mind a fox salivating at the hen house before ripping into his prey.

Her resolve not to meet with him crumbled when he told her she could name a public place in which to meet with him in the light of day—and such a meeting could make her a hundred quid richer. *A hundred quid!* It took her more than half a year of working six nights a week to earn that much money. The least she could do was listen to what the man had to say.

She suspected he might have designs on her. Along with the other hostesses—all hired for their beauty—she was accustomed to being admired by the patrons.

One thing was for certain. There wasn't enough money in all of England to induce her to become this lecherous man's fancy piece. She would rather grovel for crumbs in a debtor's prison.

At noon, she saw him making his way across Sydney Gardens toward her. Her heartbeat drummed. If Beelzebub inhabited Bath, she fancied he would be possessed of pitch-black hair with pale green eyes set in a strikingly white, white face. Like Henry Wolf's. She shuddered.

"Ah, Miss Macintosh, you have done me the goodness of meeting with me here today," he said by way of greeting her.

Careful not to offer her hand as she did not want to touch this sinister man, she merely nodded. She began to have an even worse feeling about this meeting. Why had she come? He wouldn't be requesting this *tête-à-tête* were his proposal noble. "What is it I must do for the hundred guineas?" she asked.

"All I am asking is that you cheat."

Why would he want her to cheat? Henry Wolf was a very rich man already. Her chest rose and fell. "I 'ave no idea how to go about cheating."

"Oh, but I think you do. That's why I selected you, Ellie. You've been at Mrs. Starr's longer than any of the other girls. I know Mrs. Starr has shown you how to mark certain cards. I'm only asking that you use your considerable expertise to help me."

Her eyes widened. "But you're a wealthy man, Mr. Wolf. I could lose me job for 'elping you."

"But you wouldn't be helping me to win, Ellie. You'd be helping another man to lose."

She swallowed. Perhaps she wouldn't lose her job for that. If a man lost, Mrs. Starr would just become richer. And happier.

Still, it was a wicked thing to do. Her eyes met his. At the sight of those chilling eyes, she looked back down. "Is there a particular man you want me to cheat?"

"Indeed there is. I mean to destroy Lord Appleton."

She gasped. "Lord Appleton! But he's so nice . . . everyone admires him. He's a great favorite."

A look of sheer evil crossed his face, and his voice was guttural when he spoke. "I will make it two hundred if you put a little potion in his drink."

"I am not going to poison Lord Appleton!"

"I'm not asking you to. The potion won't hurt him. It will merely cloud his judgment, making it easier for you to see that he loses. I mean to ruin him."

Even though she was sickened by repulsion toward this man, she managed a defiant look. "And if I don't?"

"I will ensure that Mrs. Starr throws you out on

the street. What else are you fit for, Ellie?"

Tears welled in her eyes as she shook her head.

He pressed a fistful of coins into her hands. Then he gave her one more thing. A ladies' ring. Ornately scrolled silver enclosed its large blue stone. "Lift the stone, Ellie," he commanded.

The stone lifted on a tiny hinge, and a small amount of dark liquid sloshed inside its hidden receptacle.

"You should be able to slip a few of those drops into Appleton's brandy without anyone seeing you."

Now she knew how Judas must have felt.

Chapter 1

Forrester Timothy Appleton, recently elevated to Viscount Appleton, looked up at his closest friend through bleary eyes.

"What the devil's so bloody important that you summoned me . . ." Sir Elvin drew a deep breath, "*before* noon on a Sunday morning?"

"You must prevent me from blowing my brains out." Appleton eyed the pistol on the table beside the bed from which he had not yet extracted himself.

Elvin's gaze shifted from the pearl-handled pistol to his disheveled friend. "Why, pray tell, would you be wanting to kill yourself?"

"Because ever since the death of my brother, I've shown myself to be unworthy of his title, and now I've ruined my family."

"How could you possibly have ruined your family?"

Appleton's eyes watered. "Quite easily. Last night at Mrs. Starr's I gambled away every farthing to my name . . ." His voice splintered as if he were about to break down like a woman. "I even wagered and lost this house. Killing myself would be less painful than knowing I've failed my sisters."

Sir Elvin said not a word, but calmly crossed the chamber to the bedside table. He removed the pistol, then collapsed into a chair facing his friend's bed, shaking his head in a most forlorn fashion. "Colossal catastrophe. Bloody colossal."

Neither man spoke for a moment. Appleton felt even worse. By requesting Elvin's presence here this morning, he'd hoped for a glimmer of encouragement.

Finally his friend spoke. "And you've got three more sisters to launch? And dower. Have you nothing left?"

Not the encouraging words he'd hoped to hear. Appleton slowly shook his head.

"I don't understand. You enjoy gaming as much as the next fellow, but you've never lost your head before—even after you inherited and had rather plump pockets. It ain't your personality to be totally without reason."

"It must have been the drink."

"It's not as if you can't hold your spirits. Why, you've always been able to remain upright when the rest of us were sprawled under the table."

"I don't know what came over me last night. I must have been a pathetic toss pot. Got no memory of it. I remember sitting down at Ellie's table. . ."

Elvin wiggled his brows. "Ellie's a fetching little thing."

Appleton nodded. "The next thing I remember is waking up here when Bertram brought me a message." He drew a deep breath. "You will never guess who the message was from."

His face pensive, Sir Elvin raised a brow.

"Penguin."

"What did that blighter Henry Wolf want from you?"

"It seems he's in possession of my IOUs."

Appleton shook his head in a most forlorn fashion. "That was how I learned of my ruin."

Sir Elvin's brows scrunched together. "Are you sure about the house? You lost it, too?"

Appleton could retch at the thought, but there was nothing left to empty. "According to Penguin's note."

"I should have been there." Sir Elvin frowned. "Fact is, I promised my sister I'd accompany her to one of those beastly musicals last night. So sorry, old fellow. I feel like I've let you down."

A light tap sounded at the chamber door, and the Appleton butler stepped into the room. "A Mr. Wolf to see you, my lord."

The two friends exchanged distasteful glances. "Have him wait in the library, then send Digby up to make me presentable."

"He's probably here to gloat over your misfortune. He's always hated all of us—you, George, Blanks, me and my twin—because we had bonds of friendship, and he had no friends whatsoever."

"Nothing's changed in that respect. Even with all his money, Penguin couldn't buy a friend." Appleton winced as he rose from the bed. "He's got even more reason to hate me."

Sir Elvin's eyes narrowed. "Why?"
"I gave him the cut direct."

"When was this? Why haven't I heard about it?"

"It happened in London. At Almack's. He'd spent the better part of the night watching Annie, and when he walked toward me and my sisters, I knew he meant to ask for an introduction."

"Course you couldn't introduce your sister to a man like Wolf!"

"Exactly. That's why I had to give him the cut

direct. Turned my back to him."

"Good for you! I wouldn't let him within ten feet of my sisters. Not after that business in Windsor."

* * *

A clean shave, freshly starched cravat, and finely tailored clothing could do little to compensate for Appleton's bloodshot eyes, throbbing head, or his oppressive melancholy as he and Sir Elvin strode into the walnut-paneled library half an hour later. The emerald velvet draperies had been opened to reveal a day as gloomy as he felt.

When Henry Wolf rose to greet him, Appleton would have cast up the contents of his stomach—had he not already done so these past several hours until not a drop remained.

Wolf's thick black mane and caterpillar eyebrows contrasting with pasty white skin accounted for the nickname Penguin. Appleton's good manners had prevented him from actually addressing the fellow in such a disparaging way. Still, there was no love lost between the two.

Though Appleton prided himself on his courtliness, it was impossible for him to be civil to Henry Wolf now. Appleton had only to recall how the foul creature had ruthlessly stolen the innocence of a young Windsor maiden when they were Etonians.

The Wolf family fortune had insulated him from any penalties for his wrongdoings, but Appleton and his friends had long memories, a disgust of abusing maidens—and a disdain for evading justice.

Appleton crossed the small chamber and came face to face with the visitor, who was the same height as he. "You wished to see me?"

Wolf reached into his well-cut black jacket and withdrew a handful of IOUs from Mrs. Starr's. "Yes. I purchased these from the proprietress of Bath's finest gaming establishment. I believe one of them is for the ownership of the very house in which we now stand." His malevolent pale green eyes repulsed Appleton.

How in the devil was Appleton to get these back when he'd lost everything? Had Wolf come here solely to take pleasure in his misery? "I did not know you had a fancy to live in my house and displace not only me but also my three unmarried sisters."

"My good man, you misjudge me. I've come to help you. In fact, I should like to *give* all these back to you. It would be as if last night never happened."

Henry Wolf was incapable of helping anyone except himself. He would push his own mother off a bridge if she prevented his passage. "I never took you for the benevolent sort, old fellow."

"Ah, but you have something I want."

Of course. Appleton's eyes widened. He failed to see what he could possibly have that Henry Wolf would want. "I am perfectly willing to hear you out, but I think you must be mistaken."

Wolf moved toward the fire. His shiny black Hessians abutted the gleaming brass fender surrounding the hearth..

"Would you care to sit?" Appleton asked. "Can I offer you Madera?"

"Nothing to drink, but I will sit."

Wolf sat on one end of the emerald sofa that faced the fire and Elvin at the other end. Appleton seated himself in a large, armchair near the fire and faced the man he loathed.

The notion that there might be some way to reclaim this house lifted Appleton's spirits, but he knew Wolf could not be trusted. What game was he playing? Appleton tried to think of things that he might be asked to do, services which might need to be performed in exchange for the return of the IOUs.

Perhaps this friendless man merely wanted an introduction into the Bath society where Appleton and his friends mingled so easily. For such a reward, Appleton could put aside his dislike of Wolf and take him to the Upper Assembly Rooms.

Just as long as he kept away from Appleton's sisters.

Appleton heaved a sigh. "So. . . what can I do in order to regain ownership of our house?" He was careful to say *our* instead of *my*. He knew Wolf hated him. Perhaps Appleton's sisters' plight might elicit a more sympathetic ear.

"I should like the hand of your sister Annie in marriage."

Elvin gasped.

Appleton felt as if a saber plunged into him as he leapt to his feet and drilled Wolf with hatred in his eyes. "Never!"

A slow, sadistic smile on his chalk white face, Wolf rose from the sofa. "You have four weeks in which to decide if you'll accept me for your sister's husband or lose everything except that pile in remote Shropshire, where I assure you, those sisters of yours will die old maids."

Appleton would rather them die old maids than be united to the devil himself.

Wolf stalked toward the door.

"Do I have four weeks in which to buy back my debts from you?"

Wolf turned. "I know you have no more money, and none of your friends can get their hands on that much in four weeks."

Appleton nodded. "That's true. It's a million to one, but last night proved I'm a gambler."

"Very well. You've got four weeks. With one caveat."

Appleton lifted a brow.

"I will demand an introduction to Annie."

It was a moment before Appleton could answer. "One dance and one dance only Tuesday night at the Upper Assembly Rooms." He would make sure Annie, his favorite sister, was well apprised of Henry Wolf's ineligibility.

But he'd not tell her about the bizarre proposal. Annie was just tender hearted enough to try to sacrifice herself for her brother.

* * *

Even though Sir Elvin Steffington was his closest friend—and only other friend who was still a bachelor—Appleton still got Elvin mixed up with his twin, Melvin. If they had not appeared to be identical duplicates of one another, the brothers would never have been taken for twins, owing to the vast differences in their personalities. Bookish, scholarly Melvin had not discovered women until he was nearing thirty while Sir Elvin abhorred books and was considered by many to be Bath's resident rake—along with Appleton.

Both Steffington twins and their friend Gregory Blankenship, known as Blanks, were ensconced with Appleton in the Blankenship library to discuss Appleton's seemingly hopeless situation.

"It seems the easiest solution is to just let Annie marry the man," one of the twins said. That's when Appleton knew without a doubt the speaker was Melvin.

Three sets of eyes stared at the younger twin as if he had just escaped from Bedlam.

"Do you not remember what Penguin did to that innkeeper's young daughter in Windsor?" his brother demanded.

Melvin screwed up his mouth. "You know I wasn't interested in petticoats when I was at Eton."

"He could never get his nose out of a book for long enough," Blanks mumbled.

His twin shrugged. "I would never allow one of our sisters to associate with Henry Wolf, and Appleton feels the same about his sisters."

"The man is unfit to be in the same chamber with respectable ladies," Appleton said. "I feel beastly that I'm even going to allow Penguin to dance once with Annie, but at least it will be beneath the glow of five huge chandeliers amidst hundreds of spectators."

"And we'll all be there to offer protection," Sir Elvin offered.

Melvin eyed Appleton. "So if you don't allow Annie to marry this vile man, you have four weeks in which to raise an exceedingly vast amount of money? Is that correct?"

Appleton nodded.

"A pity none of us can get our hands on anything near the amount of money you need." Blanks frowned. "Buying Jonathan's house took every guinea I could get my hands on."

"But. . ." Melvin smiled. "There may be a solution."

Three sets of eyes riveted to the scholarly twin.

"You've got four weeks in which to woo and wed an heiress."

Appleton harrumphed. "Normally, I would have been opposed to such a plan, but I don't deserve personal happiness after what I've done. I could sacrifice myself for my family. Pity of it, I know no heiresses."

"Actually . . ." Blanks' brows lowered, "just this morning Glee was speaking of some dreadful . . . er, unfortunate heiress who's come to Bath with her ailing father. Glee felt rather sorry for her because she has no friends, and she's . . . well she's rather peculiar. They call her the Cat Lady because she goes nowhere without carrying around a cat."

Elvin brightened. "Yes! I've heard of her, too. They say she's the only child of some vastly wealthy landowner who's to settle eight hundred a year on her."

Four sets of eyes widened.

Such a woman would indeed answer his needs, but at the same time the very notion sickened him. *An unfortunate cat woman.* He would wager—though he was never going to wager again—there were other reasons a woman with a vast fortune was still unwed, and he suspected these reasons had much to do with a most unpleasant appearance.

Was she fat? Or perhaps her figure resembled a flagpole. He wasn't certain which he would prefer. He wondered if she stunk. Or could she be possessed of a hideously ugly face?

Regardless of her shortcomings, he should put his own feelings aside and be willing to forego his own happiness as penance for his wrongdoing. After all, he was now head of the Appleton family. For the first time in his thirty years, he had others to care for. He must put their needs before his own. "Pray, what is this woman's name?"

Blanks looked perplexed. "Hmmmm. Her surname is uncommon. I cannot recall it."

Elvin nodded. "There's a Pank in there, I do believe."

"I believe you're right!" Blanks said.

"Like Pankcrest or something to that effect?" Appleton asked.

"Very like that , I'd say." Elvin eyed Blanks.

Blanks screwed up his mouth. "But not quite."

"I supposed if one were to lolly about the Pump Room day in and day out, one could meet her." Appleton was resigned to his melancholy fate. "One would know her by the cat she'd be clutching."

"Excellent plan," Melvin said. "It is to be hoped you're enamored of felines, old fellow."

Appleton frowned. "I'm a dog person."

"Pity."

* * *

"Would you bring me a rug, love," Westmoreland Pankhurst asked his daughter. "It's getting colder in this chamber."

Dorothea stroked the black-and-white cat that curled upon her lap, loudly purring. "The physician said it would do you good to walk more, Papa."

"But my gout's flaring up today."

Today it was the gout. Yesterday it was his back. The day before it was a throbbing head. Sighing, she lifted the cat and set it on the Turkey carpet. "Here you go, Fur Blossom. Duty calls."

She stood and eyed her silver-haired father, who sat before the fire, one foot propped on a stool three feet from the hearth. He had begun to remind her of an Oriental potentate who lay about being waited upon. He needed only curly-toed slippers and a turban to complete the picture of total indolence.

She took him a thick woolen rug and covered his lower extremities. "Perhaps this will keep your foot from burning. It's far too close to the fire."

"Be a dear and get me one thing more," he said.

Her eyes narrowed. "Let me guess. A glass of brandy."

"Ah, my daughter is clairvoyant."

She was neither physician nor apothecary, but she believed her father's affinity for strong spirits contributed to his health problems. After she offered him the drink, she returned to her favorite reading—the *Bath Chronicle*—this time putting her white cat, Preenie Queenie, on her lap, but after a few minutes she tossed the cat down as punishment for clawing at the pages.

It was really the most peculiar thing the way she eagerly perused the gossip within the pages of this newspaper. She knew not a soul being mentioned. Perhaps it was because she had lived in so remote a place for the entirety of her three-and-twenty years that these snippets fascinated her. In a few short weeks she had memorized the names of many of Bath's figures of Society.

"Now that we're in a city," her father said, "it's time you see about dressing like the wealthy young woman you are. You'll never attract a husband in those old rags you persist in wearing, and you need a husband. I'm not always going to be here."

She rolled her eyes. "You're but nine-and-forty, Papa. I declare, you speak as if you're twice that age—though I daresay you're beginning to act it, too!"

"Would that I enjoyed more robust health," her father said in his most martyred voice.

"I'm willing to make a pact with you, Papa. I will see a dressmaker if you will walk there with me."

"The lure to see you in lovely clothing with men clamoring for your attention is very strong." Mr. Pankhurst sighed. "I suppose I could force myself to endure so exhausting an excursion for you."

She tossed her head back and laughed. Love was, indeed, blind. The likelihood of men falling prostrate over her was ridiculous. Nothing about her could possibly elevate her above average. "How am I to even meet young men?"

"You could go to the assemblies this town is noted for."

"By myself?"

"Perhaps you'll meet other young people. I feel bad I've kept you to myself all these years at Blandings with no exposure to anyone close to your own age."

"I've had you, and I've had my cats. I didn't need anyone else."

Mr. Pankhurst shook his head solemnly, tenderness in his eyes that were the same shade of brown as hers. "I can't chance exposure to damp, rainy weather with my delicate health, but if it's dry tomorrow, I *will* walk with you to the dressmaker's."

Chapter 2

The following day proved to be dry, though very cold. That her father consented to walk along the streets of Bath on so cool a morning surprised her. Even though the city was populated by many invalids, the chilly weather did not deter them on this gray November day.

A variety of conveyance, from milk carts to hackneys to young bucks showing off prized horseflesh, crowded the narrow streets, and the pavement was equally congested with throngs of pedestrians, some being pushed on the uneven pavement in invalid chairs and many of them in sedan chairs borne by sturdy men. The more robust were making their way toward the Pump Room for the obligatory drink of the nasty water said to have medicinal properties.

Dot had not yet been to the Pump Room during the three weeks they had resided in this watering city. She knew from reading the *Bath Chronicle* that the fashionable gathered there daily, and she was well aware of how exceedingly unfashionable she was in her wardrobe, which consisted of worn sprigged muslin gowns that had served her well since she'd left the school room several years previously.

Not only did she lack fashionable attire, she also was void of social graces. How could she possibly know how to mingle with young gentlemen and ladies when she'd spent her entire life buried in remote Lincolnshire with only her father and her kitties for companionship?

She did not in the least miss the comforting familiarity of the only home she'd ever known. The vibrancy of Bath invigorated her. The beauty of the city's graceful, uniform architecture of golden stone mesmerized her. She'd actually crossed the River Avon on a bridge that resembled a street with shops on either side and nary a view of the river below.

Even the hawkers on the pavement attempting to entice passersby with posies and ill-dressed men selling penny pamphlets fascinated her.

As they drew nearer the pit of roasting chestnuts, she was tempted by the pleasant aroma. "Have you ever tasted roasted chestnuts?" she asked her father.

Fur Blossom, whom Dot carried in her arms, must also have been attracted by the smell because she launched herself from her mistress's arms, leaping toward the steaming chestnut pit—just as a huge dog of indeterminate breed had the same notion.

Dot's scream pierced the air as she surged after her cat. Terrified, she feared the dog would devour the fleet Fur Blossom before Dot could reach her.

The dog's attention quickly shifted from the hot nuts to the cat leaping toward the pit. The dog growled viciously and lunged toward Fur Blossom.

Just as the dog's open mouth was about to clamp down on the unfortunate cat, a man's hand swooped down and lifted the hissing cat away.

But not without injury to himself. Scarlet trickled from the man's wrist.

Dot's mouth gaped open as she beheld the brave hero who had snatched Fur Blossom from the teeth of a horrid death. It was as if this man had stepped from the pages of a tale of knights of yore. She'd never seen such a magnificent specimen of manhood.

The woman beside him shouted. "You've hurt yourself!" She tried to examine the flesh wound.

The man, who Dot judged to be around thirty, brushed her aside. "Pray, don't make such a fuss."

Dot raced to retrieve her frightened cat from the man. "My dear sir, I am wholeheartedly in your debt for saving the life of my precious kitty." She took Fur Blossom and held her close while eyeing the handsome man. He needed but a suit of armor to be a gallant knight. "I feel wretched you've been hurt."

The man's mossy-coloured eyes drilled her.

He had every right to be angry with her. After all, her cat had put him into jeopardy. That vicious dog could have dealt him serious injury. It could even have killed him.

He began to address her. "You must be . . ."

Mr. Pankhurst walked up and shook hands with Fur Blossom's savior. "I'm Westmoreland Pankhurst, and this is my daughter, Dorothea. We are, indeed, in your debt, my good man."

The man's eyes flashed with mirth.

How could he act so amused when his wrist must be stinging like the devil?

"It's a pleasure to make your acquaintance," the man said to her father. "I'm Lord Appleton, and this is my sister, Annie Appleton."

Lord Appleton! Dot had read about the rake in the *Bath Chronicle*! The man was a profligate. He was known to hang about Mrs. Starr's gaming establishment, and it was even hinted that he kept a mistress! She could not remove her gaze from him. In her three-and-twenty years she had never had the opportunity to see what a profligate looked like.

She hadn't expected one to be so fine looking. Though she was no arbiter of taste, she believed Lord Appleton was possessed of an unerring sense of fashion, as was his sister. He wasn't exceedingly tall, but he was taller than average. Both siblings shared the same cork brown hair and green eyes, and both were fair.

She had never felt so dowdy. It wasn't just her clothing. Miss Appleton was fashionably fair and even though it was an overcast day, she wore the mandatory bonnet. Dot never wore bonnets. Because she had never made the effort to protect her skin from the sun, it was unfashionably bronzed. She was quite certain the skin on her face resembled a well-worn saddle. It was not creamy and smooth like Miss Appleton's.

"It's lovely to meet you," Miss Appleton said, moving closer and reaching to pet Fur Blossom. "What a beautiful cat! Do tell me, what is his name?"

"*Her* name is Fur Blossom." Dot looked up at his lordship. "I do apologize for my cat's actions, for endangering you." Then without thinking and completely forgetting that she was addressing a profligate who was also an aristocrat. "You were very brave. I'm incredibly indebted to you, my lord." As she spoke, she noticed the blood had saturated the snowy white of his shirt cuff.

She handed her cat to her father, keeping the little cat blanket she'd wrapped Fur Blossom in, and raced to Lord Appleton's side. She tenderly lifted his forearm and wrapped it in the miniature blanket and attempted to staunch the flow of blood. "My father will insist on replacing your shirt, my lord, and I beg that you see an apothecary."

He shook his head. "It's nothing."

"It's *not* nothing."

His gaze softened. "All will be well, Miss Pankhurst, if you and your father will do me the goodness of accompanying my sister and me to the Pump Room this morning."

She stiffened. She did not want to be inhospitable, especially after what he had done for her—and Fur Blossom. Her eyes darted to Miss Appleton. "But Miss Appleton looks so lovely, and I . . . do not."

"We've just arrived from the country," Mr. Pankhurst explained. "My daughter and I were just on the way to the dressmaker's. She's to have a new wardrobe."

Lord Appleton's gaze whisked over her. "She's delightfully charming just as she is. A breath of country air."

"Oh, please, I implore you to come with us," Miss Appleton urged. "Bath is so thin right now. I'm frightfully in need of friends. My beastly sisters have deserted me and gone to Weymouth."

Already reeling from Lord Appleton's referring to her as *delightfully charming*, Dot was flattered to think this lovely young woman wanted to be friends with her. She'd never had a friend before. "I fear I'll be an embarrassment to you both."

"Never!" Lord Appleton said. Then he did a most peculiar thing. He offered her his arm. Her heartbeat exploded. She trembled as she settled her hand on his proffered arm and began to walk beside him. Had she done that correctly? Was there a right way or a wrong way?

She worried if she'd trip and fall on her face. What other ways could she embarrass this well-mannered man, who happened to be a nobleman—and a profligate?

He might be a seasoned rake, but the man *was* being exceedingly kind to her. She was neither pretty nor fashionable nor a figure in Society. How could she ever show him her appreciation?

How excited she was to finally be seeing the Pump Room about which she had read so much. And to be accompanied by the handsome Lord Appleton!

When they reached the Pump Room, her Papa gave Fur Blossom back to her. They began to stroll the massive chamber. She made some quick observations, the first being that Fur Blossom was the only animal in attendance. If she came again, she would be wise to leave her pets at home or suffer potential ridicule.

A few hundred people strolled the impressive room—more people than she had ever seen inside of a single building before. Other than those lined up for the small queue to obtain their cups of water, most of the attendees were circling the lofty room, and a small orchestra provided soothing music.

It soon became obvious to her that others were staring at them. It must be a peculiar sight to see the fashionable Appletons accompanied by so dowdy a country miss. Dot knew enough from reading the *Bath Chronicle* to know that Lord Appleton was a highly sought-after bachelor. And now she understood why. What lady would not be attracted to him?

As they circled the chamber, she counted more than a dozen lovely young ladies far more suited than she to be walking beside the attractive young peer.

She felt even dowdier when his lordship stopped to introduce her to two beautiful sisters who were married to friends of his. A stunning copper-headed Mrs. Glee Blankenship was married to his life-long friend whom they all referred to as Blanks, and her sister was Mrs. Felicity Moreland, a graceful blonde. Dot wondered what their husbands looked like because both women were so extraordinarily lovely, and their welcoming manners matched their beauty.

"Please, Miss Pankhurst," Mrs. Blankenship said, "may we pay you a morning call?"

Her father stepped in. "I believe I speak for my daughter when I say she would be delighted, but she would prefer that you wait until her new clothing is delivered. We've just arrived from the country—where such finery as you ladies display was not available."

Dot nodded. She'd never thought she would ever care a whit about clothing. Until today. It was suddenly important that Lord Appleton see her more favorably. She would never be as beautiful as these sisters were or as lovely as Miss Appleton, but for the first time in her life, Dot looked forward to having fashionable clothes.

The two sisters took their leave to continue around the chamber, and Lord Appleton and her father went to fetch them water. Bath's famed medicinal water. "You know, Miss Pankhurst," Miss Appleton said, "I don't mean to offend you, but I have noticed that you and I are the same size, and it would mean a great deal to me if you would accompany me to the Upper Assembly Rooms tonight. You could wear one of my dresses."

Dot froze. "But you see, I have never learned how to dance. I've never had any need to do so."

Miss Appleton nodded slowly. "You simply must come back to our house. My brother and I can teach you enough to get by tonight. You don't have to dance with anyone save Timothy."

Dot assumed Timothy was Lord Appleton.

When Lord Appleton returned and offered her the water, she sipped it, grimacing. "It's nasty!" she exclaimed.

Lord Appleton chuckled as he shook his head. "Observe that I did not partake."

"I can certainly see why," Mr. Pankhurst said. "I can now say that I've tried it. For the first and last time!"

"But, Papa, it might help your infirmities."

Her father rolled his eyes. "I shall take my chances."

Lord Appleton offered her his arm. "I beg that you do me the goodness of walking about the chamber with me, Miss Pankhurst."

Because she put her right hand on his sleeve, she hitched Fur Blossom over her shoulder almost as if she were a sack of grain, pressing her left hand to her back. To her mortification, half way around the chamber, her cat leapt from her arms and scurried across the floor.

When she brushed against Glee Blankenship's skirts, that poor lady tumbled to the floor. Lord Appleton rushed to help her up while Dot raced after her errant cat. Every time she got near the animal, the feline sped forward. Dot's speed was no match for the exasperating cat.

"Fur Blossom!" she called in her most commanding voice. But it was rather like speaking to a brick wall. The cat definitely had a mind of its own.

As she sped to and fro, everyone in the room had come to a complete standstill, and most of them were heartily chuckling.

She quit calling after the cat, not that it would in the least diminish her humiliating position. Nor would it wipe away the burn in her cheeks.

Now Lord Appleton joined in the mission to corner her wayward cat. As Fur Blossom ran away from Dot, his lordship ran toward them. This succeeded in trapping the black and white cat in a corner where Dot promptly launched herself at it.

This time she managed to hook her hands into the cat's sizable belly—but not without sprawling over the wooden floor in a most unladylike fashion. She chided Fur Blossom because she was too humiliated to look up at his lordship. She didn't think she could bear to look up at him at the precise moment. No doubt, he would be eyeing her with pity. She could not bear it.

Her father came up just then, his brows lowering. "I think, Dot, in the future it would be wise to leave your cats at home."

He didn't need to tell her. Nothing had ever humiliated Dot more. Onlookers were still giggling.

She finally looked up at Lord Appleton. "Forgive me, my lord. I'm unaccustomed to town ways."

His face softened. "There's nothing to forgive. Can I assist with your cat?"

Mr. Pankhurst intervened. "I think I'll take Fur Blossom home. As it is, I'm tired and need to return home. I understand you're going to the

Appletons' house from here."

"I ought to go with you." She could not inflict her embarrassing presence upon the Appletons anymore. They deserved better.

"You'll do no such thing!" Miss Appleton said. "You promised you'd come home with us."

So she could further humiliate herself with her ignorance of dancing. "Perhaps I shouldn't."

Lord Appleton bent down and helped her up. "We must insist, Miss Pankhurst. My sister is prostrate with no friends."

Just like Dot, who had no friends. She looked at Miss Appleton's hopeful gaze. And even though Dot thoroughly understood the peculiarity of her own behavior today, she believed that the Appletons accepted her as she was. What wonderful people they were.

Lord Appleton regarded her father. "Since you know nothing of us, I am sure you'd like to ensure your daughter's reputation. Please, Mr. Pankhurst, come home with us." He eyed Fur Blossom. "That cat will be most welcome." He eyed his sister. "My sister is enchanted with the creature."

* * *

It was a rather arduous walk, mostly uphill, to the Appletons' residence on Camden Crescent. Dot was most proud of her father for not once complaining.

The house was everything she could have expected from a home belonging to a peer. It was considerably larger than the one her father had taken. Its situation at the street's center point accentuated its stateliness in much the same way as symmetrically arranged chairs on either side of a throne.

The interiors, while of grand proportions and featuring furnishings that had once been magnificent, indicated this was a home to a large family that lived over every inch. Copies of Ackermann's and books with slips of paper marking the pages piled up on tables, and the whist table that had been set up in front of the fire in the drawing room awaited a new gathering of players. A half-filled cup of tea had not been removed from the top of the pianoforte. Without asking, Dot knew there was no Lady Appleton. The house needed a matriarch's touch.

After the Appleton servants rolled up the carpet in the drawing room, Lord Appleton attempted to teach Dot some dance steps while his sister provided music on the pianoforte.

Mr. Pankhurst watched the proceedings from the chair he had collapsed in after the vigorous walk, holding Fur Blossom for his daughter.

"Even if I could still remember the steps after five-and-twenty years," Dot's father said, sighing. "I wouldn't be able to teach her, owing to the ever-mounting abundance of my infirmities."

"But I daresay you're still a young man," Miss Appleton said.

"You do look fit," Lord Appleton added.

Mr. Pankhurst's lids lowered as he sighed. For the second time. "Would that it were so. Only for my daughter—who is possessed of every benevolent attribute a girl could have, along with a high degree of intelligence—would I be able to endure so taxing a walk as I've undertaken today."

Dot glared at him. "You did very well, Papa, but, pray, do not boast on me. Can you not see how poorly I compare to Miss Appleton?"

"Fiddlefudge!" Mr. Pankhurst eyed the female

hostess. "I mean no disparagement to you, Miss Appleton, but anyone with eyes in their head can see that Dot here—or Dorothea, which is her given name—is a pretty little thing, even if she doesn't wear stylish dresses. Yet."

"Of course," Lord Appleton agreed, offering Dot his hand. "May I have the honor of the next set, Miss Pankhurst?"

Learning new things had always come easily to Dot. Yet today she was embarrassed over her lack of even the most rudimentary vocabulary of dance. Imagine the French words *chassé* referring to a dance move! How would she ever learn all there was to learn?

Another impediment was her physical awkwardness. While his lordship, though a man, performed the dance steps gracefully, Dot felt like a clomping elephant.

Her gracious host and hostess never let on that they saw her deficiencies. "Very good, Miss Pankhurst," Lord Appleton complimented when she executed one of the steps he'd shown her.

"I declare," Miss Appleton said, "Miss Pankhurst is possessed of a natural talent for dancing."

Blushing, Dot's gaze swept from brother to sister. "You two are great prevaricators."

"They most certainly are not," her father defended. "You, my dear daughter, are a quick learner. Always have been." He addressed their host. "Her old governess said of all the girls she'd instructed in thirty years, my Dot was the quickest learner and the most intelligent of all."

Dot's cheeks burned. "I beg that you not praise me so, Papa. The Appletons will think *you* a great prevaricator."

As self-conscious as she was over her ineptitude, Dot was even more rattled every time Lord Appleton's hand touched hers. How could so simple a touch affect her so profoundly? It seemed to rob her of breath while sending pulsating charges all the way to her toes. More than that, an odd sense of well-being suffused her each time his hand grasped hers, each time his warm eyes settled on hers.

What had come over her? These were such strange, alien feelings.

But she could never say they were unpleasant. In spite of her embarrassment over her lack of skill, she was enjoying every moment. She was even looking forward to going to the Upper Assembly Rooms that night—just to prolong her time with her two new friends.

Once Lord Appleton deemed her skilled enough to dance with him that evening, her father and Fur Blossom departed, and she went upstairs to try on one of Miss Appleton's gowns.

"I love your bedchamber," she said. The room looked like something Miss Appleton would have selected for it reminded Dot of the lady. The papered walls featured pale yellow flowers and soft greenery on a cream background. The chamber's two tall casements were framed with the lichen-coloured draperies in silk, the same silk that enclosed the full tester bed.

Miss Appleton's maid soon brought down a pair of dresses. One was snow white, the other rose. "With your luxuriously dark hair and honeyed skin," Miss Appleton said, "I think the white will be stunning on you."

Honeyed skin sounded much better than saddle leather! How kindly Miss Appleton was.

Dot did not see how anything could be stunning on someone as unfashionably dark as she. How she longed to be as fair as Miss Appleton! But she respected this lady's opinion on matters of taste.

She tried on the white dress and stood before the cheval glass to look at herself. The woman in the looking glass looked nothing like her! Were her hair arranged with any degree of competence—something Dot lacked—that woman might look . . . well, attractive.

Her gaze lowered to her breasts. So much of her breasts had never shown before. She wondered if Miss Appleton's were as large as hers, for Dot's looked far fuller than most young women's. Colour rose to her cheeks.

Of course, she could not be seen like this.

"Oh, Miss Pankhurst, I was right! You *are* stunning. My brother's apt to be rapturously captivated by you!"

Dot's face grew even hotter. The notion of Lord Appleton noticing *that* part of her body mortified her. And she could never *captivate* a fine man like him! "You *are* a very great prevaricator, Miss Appleton."

The lady shook her head adamantly. "You *are* most lovely. You positively must wear this tonight!"

"But look at . . ." Dot could not bring herself to mention that part of her anatomy. "At the immodesty!"

Miss Appleton tossed her head back and laughed. "All the women will be displaying themselves in such a manner tonight. It's just that Nature has most kindly endowed you. Never be embarrassed by that. Men admire women with bounteous chests."

"But my Papa!"

"Your father will swell a hundredfold with pride that his daughter is so singularly admired." Miss Appleton came closer and lifted the back of Dot's hair. "You must have your maid fashion your hair in the Grecian style."

Dot felt embarrassed once again. "But I have no maid." Papa had been insisting that she needed a maid now that she was in Bath, and she kept insisting that she didn't.

"Then you must use mine. Just for tonight. Please say you'll stay here. My maid can dress your hair. You'll be astonishingly beautiful."

"I have already been such an imposition on you."

"Not at all. It's fun having you here since my sisters are visiting our cousins in Weymouth. I didn't like to leave Timothy alone. He still feels dreadful about inheriting after the death of our eldest brother, whom we lost just this past year. He took lung fever and died at the age of two-and-thirty."

Dot's face collapsed sympathetically. "My mother died of lung fever at four-and-twenty. Papa took it hard. He's never remarried."

"How old were you?"

"I was almost three."

"I don't suppose you even remember her?"

Dot shook her head. "Not at all. It's always been just me and Papa. And my cats."

Miss Appleton then settled her hand upon Dot's. "Now you're going to have new friends."

Miss Appleton and her brother were the most genuinely welcoming people she could ever imagine. How fortunate she was to have met them.

"If you're certain you don't object," Dot said, "I'll go down and send Papa and Fur Blossom home, and I'll stay here to dress for tonight's fete."

* * *

While Becca was dressing Miss Pankhurst's hair, Appleton requested a word with his sister, and then closed the door to his library behind them. She looked queerly at him. "What's all the secrecy about?"

"I beg a private word with you. That's all. Please." He waved her toward the emerald sofa. "Sit before the fire. It's been beastly cold today."

"Unless one is dancing."

He smiled as he came to sit beside her. "You have an admirer who's persuaded me to introduce you to him tonight."

"And?"

"And he will request a dance."

She nodded.

"You may dance with him once, and once only. Without going into particulars, allow me to say the man is unworthy of you."

"What is the man's name?"

His lips compressed, a distasteful look on his face. "Henry Wolf."

"From where is it you know him?"

"Eton."

"Was he a friend to you and Sir Elvin and Lord Sedgewick and the others?"

He shook his head. "I wouldn't say any of us were friends with him. Acquaintances."

"How does he know me?"

Appleton shrugged. "I believe he once admired you at Almack's."

Annie had much to recommend her. Many, many men had been attracted to her loveliness. And her attributes did not stop with the physical. She came from a high-born family, was possessed of a sweet nature, and displayed uncommon good sense. She also demonstrated persistently excellent taste in all she did, but especially in her selection of dress. His sister was close to perfection. Far, far too good for most men, but most especially for the likes of Henry Wolf.

He drew a deep breath. "There's one more matter about which I must speak to you."

She turned to face him, a quizzing look on her sweet face.

"This is difficult for me to say. You see, I've . . . had a financial setback and find that I must marry an heiress."

Her brows lowered. "You mean you cannot marry for love?"

He tossed his head aside. "What do I care for love? Love is for poets—and women!" He had always hoped he might one day fall in love in the same way as had his friends—friends like Blanks with his Glee. And even Melvin and Catherine. Melvin had never noticed women—until he'd fallen in love with the pretty young widow.

Appleton recalled George, Lord Sedgewick, had not married Sally Spencer for love, but they soon fell quite desperately in love with each other. And the Morelands! Thomas and Felicity adored each other. Even that confirmed bachelor Jonathan Blankenship was now happily married to that bookish Mary Arbuckle, to whom he was so well suited, and the two acted perfectly silly toward each other.

Appleton had stayed a bachelor all these years

because he was waiting for a love match like his friends had found.

But a love match was not going to be in his future. He would still have Mrs. Pratt to warm his bed. It wasn't love, but she met certain needs.

"You simply *must* marry for love!"

His sister would have to look at the distressing situation like a female. "I am now the head of the house, and my responsibilities must come first."

Her eyes narrowed. "Forrester Timothy Appleton, have you lost your money gambling?"

He gave her a haughty look. "I may have lost a portion, but surely you don't take me for one who would completely lose his head . . ."

"Well, I will own, you've always been one for moderation."

He coughed. "It's time I marry. After all, I'm thirty. All of my friends, save one, are wed. It's time. And I choose to marry a woman with a fortune."

"But we don't know any heiresses."

"Actually, Annie. . ." He lowered his voice to a whisper, "Miss Pankhurst is an heiress. Her father's said to be vastly wealthy."

Her eyes rounded. "Forrester Timothy Appleton! Do you mean you knew all along who the lady was? That all your kindness to her was because she's an heiress? And I thought you were being such a dear to a sweet, plain girl. I was inordinately proud of you!"

He had the decency to feel beastly ashamed. "I didn't know who she was when I saved that bloody cat of hers from almost certain death—with no regard for my own well-being, I might add."

"Then how *did* you know who she was?"

He lowered his voice to a whisper again. "I had

heard that an heiress had recently arrived in Bath who just happened to be plain and who walked about with cats. I didn't have to possess the brains of Melvin Steffington to make the deduction."

His sister gave him a hostile look. "I won't have you using that poor girl. Or breaking her heart. From the way you treated her today, I—who know you well—thought you were attracted to her. So you can imagine how flattered she is by your attentions. You told her she was *delightfully charming*! You said she was *like a breath of country air*. You even agreed with her admittedly prejudiced father when he said she was pretty! I think you're being appallingly wicked."

"I thought I was kind to her. Gave up my entire afternoon. Didn't even object to escorting what had to be the plainest maiden in all of Bath around the Pump Room for all to see. My reputation as a connoisseur of beauty is destroyed." He frowned. "I even became a complete laughingstock chasing that blasted cat of hers around the Pump Room!"

"You're horrid, and I'm ashamed of you." Annie sprang from the sofa and stormed from the chamber.

* * *

While Digby assisted him into his meticulously fitted and spotless black jacket for the evening's assembly, tied his cravat, and helped him into silken stockings, Appleton felt wretched. Instead of enlisting Annie's help to win Miss Pankhurst's affections, he'd angered his sister and shamed himself.

Still, he couldn't tell Annie he was doing it for her and their sisters. If it were just him, he could have let the house in Bath go and eked by on the modest income from their small estate in Shropshire. But he had to provide for his sisters. Hefty dowries would be required for them to attract husbands suitable to their station. And the dresses and hats and gloves and all the finery three young ladies of refined taste needed! He had no choice but to marry an heiress.

Despite that cat business, Miss Pankhurst, thankfully, was not like one in her dotage. She seemed to be possessed of good sense, and he would vow that with a proper wardrobe—which her wealthy father had already promised—she would be tolerably handsome.

Fully dressed now, he stood at the foot of the stairs awaiting his sister and Miss Pankhurst when the door to Annie's chamber opened. Annie came out first. She wore a rose-coloured gown and looked her usual lovely self. Appleton sighed. A pity. That damned Wolf would be sure to be attracted to her.

Then Miss Pankhurst came into view, and Appleton almost lost his breath.

Chapter 3

Had one of the Royal Princesses begun to glide down his modest stairway, Appleton could not have been more astonished. This vision in white coming toward him looked nothing like the dowdy Miss Pankhurst with whom he'd spent the better part of the day. Why had he not been aware of the rich deep, lustrous brown of her hair? It now swept back from her face in a most elegant fashion. Her face, too, looked very fine. Perhaps not beautiful, but there was nothing to give offense.

His eye quite naturally traveled along the drape of her snowy gown but froze at her breasts. He swallowed. Why had he not noticed how . . . how bountiful they were? Full and plump and everything a man could hope to find in a woman. How had she managed to conceal them? It wasn't like Appleton not to notice when a woman was possessed of such an endowment.

Good manners demanded that he remove his gawk from her chesterly assets, and as he did so, the impression she gave, descending the staircase with her dark hair and large, dark eyes set against the gown's white, reminded him of someone he'd once seen. Someone with whom he'd been favorably impressed.

Then he remembered.

At the London opera house, he'd fancied himself in love with the beautiful Italian singer Maria Cara, but none of his efforts to wrangle an introduction to the beautiful songstress ever succeeded.

Tonight, Miss Pankhurst reminded him of Maria Cara. Which explained why he'd nearly lost his breath when he'd looked up and seen her.

Escorting Miss Dorothea Pankhurst to the Upper Assembly Rooms tonight wasn't going to be anything like escorting her around the Pump Room today had been. Tonight he would *not* be a laughingstock. He fully expected to be the envy of the other bachelors in attendance.

When she reached the bottom step, he offered his arm. "My dear Miss Pankhurst, I do not exaggerate when I say that your beauty astonishes me."

She placed her hand on his proffered sleeve. "You're too kind, my lord."

This one time, she neither protested nor called him a prevaricator. She had enough good sense to have seen how lovely she looked. Unlike other young ladies schooled in maidenly coyness, artifice of any kind was alien to her.

With the new wardrobe her father's fortune could procure, along with the personal maid she would be sure to secure now that she was in Bath, it was just a matter of time before every bachelor within fifty miles picked up her scent and came panting after her.

It was imperative that he win her affections. And quickly.

In the Appleton coach, he sat across from the ladies. "Now, Miss Pankhurst, owing to your inexperience, it's best that you only dance once tonight. With me."

Annie agreed.

"For one thing, Miss Pankhurst—and I don't mean to sound didactic if you already know this—but one is not supposed to dance with a man to whom one's not been introduced," Annie said. "Therefore, we'll be careful that you're only introduced to my brother's closest friends."

"And I'll warn them away from dancing with the woman who's *my* special guest," Appleton said.

He would vow he'd made her blush, but it was difficult to tell, given the darkness in the carriage.

* * *

My beauty astonishes him. I'm to be *his* special guest. As handsome as she'd thought him that afternoon, she found him so much more so tonight that his very presence caused her to feel as if she were in one of those balloons that soared above Hyde Park.

Where he had dressed carelessly casual in the daytime, at night he wore an impeccable black coat and breeches along with snowy shirt and cravat and stockings. No man could draw more admiration at this evening's assembly. It was as if that hero from *Pride and Prejudice*, Mr. Darcy, had accompanied her.

It was a wonder Dot could communicate at all during the short coach ride to the Upper Assembly Rooms. In less than a single day she had gone from a decidedly dowdy country spinster to a beautifully dressed young woman who felt like a princess. And all because of her new friends, the Appletons. How could she ever repay their kindness?

Their presence reduced her own nervousness

over the impending assembly. Even with Papa's most insistent urging, she would have avoided the assemblies. She was in possession of enough intelligence to know how unfit she was to be accepted at such a gathering. But now that she'd been the object of the Appletons' attentions, she no longer worried that she'd be hideously ridiculed.

She might no longer be ridiculed as she must have been at the Pump Room, but she still feared the unknown. She did not want to embarrass her benefactors. Yet she knew that because of them, nothing too terrible could occur.

She cautioned herself to stay close to the lovely Miss Appleton and mimic everything that lady did. Except Miss Appleton was certain to dance every set, and Dot was not ready to do so. What would she do whilst her friend was dancing? Perhaps Lord Appleton would stay close and enlighten her on all the correct protocols.

It was exhilarating, too, to be with others so close to her age. She felt guilty for her newfound belief that coming to Bath may have been the best thing that had ever happened to her when it was Papa's ill health that had brought them here. She would have felt far more wretched if she believed her father was truly gripped by a serious illness, but she had far more confidence in his ability to heal than he did.

She turned to Miss Appleton. "I fear I've been a poor a companion. I was so dumfounded by my own transformation I neglected to say how lovely you look tonight."

Miss Appleton's gown of soft muslin only barely covered her own bosom which was significantly smaller than Dot's. It was a wonder the two ladies *could* wear the same dresses! Seeing her new friend dressed just as immodestly as she allayed Dot's discomfort. If Miss Appleton could go to the Upper Assembly Rooms dressed in such a manner, Dot was convinced all the females in attendance must reveal a similar expanse of flesh—for Miss Appleton was a pillar of propriety and good breeding. Her unblemished reputation stood up to the scrutiny of the *Bath Chronicle*, which never disparaged the viscount's pretty sister in any way.

Miss Appleton's maid styled both women's hair in the same swept-back manner, but they looked vastly different. Dot's hair was dark and thick, and her hostess's was a wispy light brown given to jut into bouncy curls.

"I daresay one as lovely as you will dance every set," Dot continued.

"My sister is always a highly sought-after dancing partner," Lord Appleton said. "She is never seated. But don't fear, Miss Pankhurst. I'll not forsake you. I'll sit with you."

"Oh, my lord, you are too kind." How fortunate she'd been to have met this wonderful man. He just could not be a profligate. He was unquestionably the most admirable man she'd ever met.

And to think, she never would have met him had it not been for Fur Blossom's naughtiness. Could she possibly end up owing her happiness to Fur Blossom?

"Ah, we're here," his lordship said.

* * *

Appleton didn't see any of his friends when they arrived. He hadn't really expected to. George, Lord Sedgewick, was not in Bath at present, and he doubted Melvin would be here. The fellow despised dancing. Perhaps later he'd see Blanks. Glee Blankenship and her sister, Felicity Moreland, enjoyed the assemblies, so their husbands might come. Appleton had made sure to arrive early enough to claim chairs in a good location, given that Miss Pankhurst would be spending most of the night watching the dancers rather than participating.

Elvin, Appleton knew, would not miss being here because he knew this was when Penguin would meet Annie. Since his distrust of Wolf was as strong as Appleton's, Sir Elvin would definitely be here to support his friend and his friend's sister.

Elvin didn't know yet that his friend had been successful in his first attempts at wooing the heiress Miss Pankhurst. Appleton smiled to himself when he thought of how surprised Elvin would be when he met her and learned that she was not some skinny, boy-chested dimwit with a basket of cats on her lap.

Appleton led the ladies to the scarlet seats, where he saved an additional one for Elvin.

"This is even larger than the Pump Room," Miss Pankhurst exclaimed. "It's like I imagine Westminster Abbey."

He chuckled and covered her hand with his. "It's much smaller than Westminster Abbey."

Her already large chocolate eyes widened even more. "You've been there?"

"Many times."

"Yes, I suppose you have often been to London."

The poor woman—for she was no longer a girl—knew no more of the world than a child.

More and more people kept filling the chamber,

and it was more difficult to be heard over the drone of voices.

He watched with amusement as Miss Pankhurst's head tilted and she looked far above at the ceiling and its five enormous crystal chandeliers sparkling with hundreds of candles illuminating the room as if it were daytime.

Like a child, she could not disguise her excitement. Her eyes shimmered, and the smile on her face looked as permanent as her aquiline nose.

Members of the orchestra took their seats and began to tune their instruments. The first set would begin in a matter of minutes. He'd decided that he should give Miss Pankhurst the opportunity to observe at least one set before he asked her to stand up with him.

From a distance, he saw that Thomas Moreland and his brother-in-law Blanks moved toward the card room. Their pretty wives were now in the ballroom, walking toward them.

He rose and greeted them.

Glee Blankenship's mouth dropped open as she gawked at Miss Pankhurst. "I declare! Can this be Miss Pankhurst? Oh, my dear lady, you are most decidedly lovely tonight."

Leave it to the outspoken Pixie to blurt out her opinions so bluntly.

Miss Pankhurst's lashes lowered. "You're so kind, Mrs. Blankenship. Thank you very much."

"But I thought you hadn't procured your new wardrobe yet," Pixie, er, Glee Blankenship said.

"Oh, I haven't." Miss Pankhurst eyed Annie. "Miss Appleton did me the goodness of allowing me to borrow one of her gowns."

"It looks as if it were made just for you." Glee's

gaze darted to him. "How fortunate you are, Lord Appleton, to be able to escort so lovely a lady here tonight."

He set a hand to Miss Pankhurst's waist. "I am well aware of my good fortune."

Mrs. Moreland, another great beauty but more reserved than her sister, looked at the chairs in front of theirs. "Is anyone sitting here?"

"We were hoping you ladies would join us," Annie answered.

Once the five of them were seated, he was relieved to see Sir Elvin enter the chamber.

His friend cordially greeted Annie and their friend George's sisters, Felicity Moreland and Glee Blankenship. Then he looked to Appleton for an introduction to the unfamiliar lady.

"Sir Elvin, might I present to you Miss Dorothea Pankhurst, who is recently in Bath from Lincolnshire."

A jolt of recognition at her name was quickly followed by a sly glance at Appleton, and then Elvin bowed and addressed Miss Pankhurst with the greatest civility. "A pleasure to meet you, Miss Pankhurst. I do hope you will honor me with a set tonight."

Appleton stiffened. "Miss Pankhurst chooses to mostly observe this evening. She's never before been to an assembly and does not wish to do anything that would invite ridicule—not that I believe she ever could."

"Oh, no. Certainly not."

Miss Pankhurst curtsied. "I am delighted to meet a friend of Lord Appleton's. Thank you for your supportive words, Sir Elvin."

How would a newcomer like Elvin gauge the lady, Appleton wondered. He would vow that someone meeting her for the first time tonight would be favorably impressed. Even though Annie should take all the credit for the transformation of the country miss, Appleton himself swelled with pride. After all, even when she had been making a spectacle of herself with that damned cat and dressing practically in rags, he had allowed all of Bath to see him escort her around the Pump Room. And act the fool, chasing that maddening feline of hers all over the Pump Room. He'd been as courteous to her as he would have been were she the offspring of a duke.

Elvin glanced at the lone empty seat. "I say, are you perchance saving that for me?"

Appleton nodded. "Indeed we are."

So now Appleton had Miss Pankhurst on one side of him with Elvin on the other. Just so that he would not be obliged to speak the whole time to Miss Pankhurst, he had ensured that Annie sat on the other side of her, though he did not expect Annie to spend very much time sitting. He had not exaggerated when he said she was one of the most popular dancing partners in all of Bath.

As soon as the two men were seated, and Annie had engaged Miss Pankhurst in conversation, Elvin whispered hoarsely in his ear. "Aren't you bloody lucky? Your heiress ain't a plain dunderhead after all. I'd say she's bang up to scratch."

Appleton remembered again how plain she had looked earlier this same day and was grateful for what her father's purse would be able to accomplish—not that tonight's appearance could be improved upon. She would never again embarrass Appleton. "It's amazing what can be had when one has a hefty purse."

Elvin's elbows poked him as a smile eked across his face. "With a figure much to your liking, I daresay."

It was well known that shapeless women held no appeal for Appleton.

"Your brother coming tonight?" Appleton asked.

"No, he's mad at work on a new book."

"I believe it's the same with Jonathan Blankenship. But Blanks is here. Moreland, too."

"In the card room?"

Appleton nodded.

"Seen Penguin yet?"

"No."

"How much does your sister know about him?"

"As little as possible."

"Only one dance with him?"

"Only one."

The orchestra started playing. Three different men rushed to Annie, and she bestowed the honor of dancing on the first to reach her chair.

As the dancing commenced, Appleton watched Miss Pankhurst. She could not remove her gaze from the groups of dancers, and that smile still had not left her face.

He had to own that there was something pretty about Miss Pankhurst. He admired her large, dark, expressive eyes very much. He liked, too, that her smile revealed fine white teeth, and she seemed to always be smiling. Or was that just because she was so vastly enjoying herself with all these sights and sounds that were new and wondrous to her?

Nevertheless, he would do everything in his power to keep that wholesome smile upon her face.

At the end of the first set, Penguin came into

the ballroom. Appleton caught a glimpse of that chalky face when the crowd parted, and Henry Wolf strode toward them, his eyes on Annie. Just the sight of the man angered Appleton.

The very notion that this man had been secretly watching his favorite sister sickened Appleton. Not about to allow him to claim the chair to which Annie was returning, he leapt to his feet to greet him. Elvin followed his lead.

After her partner restored Annie to their group, her brother was obliged to introduce her to the man who held all of his IOUs. "Annie, I should like to present to you Mr. Henry Wolf." Then, turning to Wolf, he added. "My eldest sister, Miss Annie Appleton."

Wolf bowed. "I am delighted to meet my friend's lovely sister, and I pray you will do me the goodness of standing up with me for the next set."

How dare the man claim Appleton as his friend!

His sister's uncharacteristic stiffness when she greeted Penguin pleased Appleton. "I can oblige you, sir."

That next dance, featuring a longway, was the one Appleton had practiced the most with Miss Pankhurst. After Wolf led Annie onto the dance floor, Appleton turned to his female companion. "Will you do me the honor, Miss Pankhurst?"

That bright smile faded from her face. "Would you mind awfully if I declined?"

"Of course not. My only wish is for your happiness." Oddly, he meant it.

"I shall be much happier as an observer. I think when I deem myself ready to dance, it won't be for a dance where I will be so prominently upon public display. With you being so handsome, everyone would be sure to scrutinize me, and I should perish of mortification."

Appleton was not handsome. His married friends held that distinction. But owing to the fact he was likely the most sought-after bachelor currently residing in Bath, females might be inclined to think him handsome in comparison to other, less desirable matrimonial prospects.

"I am honored by the friendship which has you mistakenly flattering me," he said, bowing his head with humility, "but it's your own beauty which demands attention from others."

He sat back down beside her and once again covered her hand with his. "I shouldn't wish to do anything which mortifies you. We'll wait. Perhaps at your next assembly we can stand up together for a country dance."

"Perhaps I will be more confident then. Papa was taking steps to engage a dancing master for me."

"Would he like a recommendation?"

Dot shook her head. "My headstrong Papa never asks like that. It's his belief that whoever is considered the most expensive must be the best."

Appleton chuckled. It must be gratifying to be as wealthy as Mr. Pankhurst.

His attention turned to Annie and Wolf as they began the slow, graceful glide down the longway formed by the two facing rows of dancers. Anyone else observing would find nothing objectionable in Henry Wolf. His dress was impeccable, and he had obviously been instructed by an extremely competent dance master. Even his interaction with Annie had been exemplary.

Were Appleton and Annie not so close, she would have been apt to think her brother daft. But Annie had always trusted him. Because of that, she would be wary of the man.

Elvin, too, watched. His elbow kept digging into Appleton's side. "Do not let her be fooled by courtly ways," he whispered hoarsely.

"You may be assured."

When Wolf escorted Annie back to her brother, he said, "May I call on you tomorrow, Miss Appleton?"

For a fraction of a second, her gaze flicked to her brother, and then returned to the man addressing her. "Alas, Mr. Wolf, I will be spending the day with Miss Pankhurst at the dressmaker's."

He fixed a smile on his face and bowed. "Perhaps another time."

At the end of the night when they assembled in his carriage, Miss Pankhurst turned to Annie. "Will you really accompany me to the dressmaker's tomorrow?"

"Neither flood nor famine could keep me away," Annie said.

"I shall be so very much in your debt. I know from reading the *Bath Chronicle*, you are one of the most fashionable women in the city."

Appleton laughed. "You mustn't believe everything you read in that rag! They'll have you believing I am a most wicked man." He shrugged. "Though I regret to say I can't claim to be worthy of being in the same coach with a fine young lady like you."

"Pray, do not listen to my brother. He is a good man. And, my dear Miss Pankhurst, don't believe everything you read of him in the *Chronicle*, either. It can be a beastly silly publication."

They delivered her to the house she and her father were letting on the Circus, and Appleton insisted on escorting her to the door where a servant in lime livery let her in.

"I am not going to see you again, my lord, until I have dresses in which I'll be fit to be seen."

"You couldn't possibly look any more charming than you look tonight." He bowed and returned to his carriage.

It was imperative that he offer for her as soon as possible. There was little doubt that Miss Pankhurst was soon to be Bath's most courted lady.

Chapter 4

"My daughter will be the prettiest girl in all of Bath in her lovely new dresses," Mr. Pankhurst said. He had insisted on accompanying her and Miss Appleton to Mrs. Gainsworth's, Dressmaker to the Fashionable, who had been enthusiastically endorsed by Miss Appleton.

She was also the most expensive in Bath—a hearty endorsement for Mr. Pankhurst.

Mrs. Gainsworth herself had shown him to a plush velvet settee where he could sit and view Dot in the various creations pinned to her in a variety of fabrics as she paraded in front of her father for approval.

"Papa! How can you say such a thing in front of Miss Appleton? She's far lovelier than I will ever be. And you're embarrassing me excessively. I beg you stop boasting about me, or I will refuse to wear a single new gown."

He looked contrite when he addressed his daughter's companion. "You must forgive me, Miss Appleton. I pray you don't fault me for being a doting father."

"Who's blind," Dot added.

"Of course not," Miss Appleton responded. "And I don't think you're blind at all. Your daughter *is* exasperatingly lovely."

Dot sighed. "You must be tired, Papa. We've

been here for more than three hours. Shall we go to the Pump Room? Perhaps a glass of the water will restore you."

He wrinkled his nose in distaste and shook his head. "I'm a very wealthy man, and even though this effort will tax my delicate health, I'm determined that you be the most fashionably dressed young lady in Bath. When we leave Mrs. Gainsworth's, we'll go to the milliner's and the glove maker's and the cobbler's and ensure that you are dressed as well as you would were your father a Royal Duke." He chuckled and lowered his voice. "Though I daresay I'm wealthier than those spendthrifts sired by our king, poor old soul that he is."

"But I'm afraid we'll drain your strength," Dot protested.

"What difference can it make whether I sit on a velvet settee here or in our house?" He effected a pained look. "I'll take care to find at least a chair wherever we go." He cast a glance at Mrs. Gainsworth. "Now tell me how many dresses will you be making for my gel?"

The matron, whose locks, a mixture of gold and silver, were shorn close to her head, began to count on her fingers. "There's the white muslin, two sprigged for morning calls, the blue with a matching pelisse, and an ivory with ermine trim and muff, another of fine silk in green. That should be enough to launch her into Bath society."

"I want each delivered to Number Five, The Circus, as each one's completed. I shall pay you in sovereigns upon every delivery. And once you have her measure and know which style she prefers, we'll want them duplicated in other colours.

Nothing will do but that my daughter be the most fashionable girl in all of Bath."

Though it was Dot's natural inclination to be embarrassed over her father's extravagance, she knew it was futile to protest.

Mrs. Gainsworth's eyes rounded, and she favored him with a beaming smile. Dot had gathered from reading the *Bath Chronicle* that many of the fashionable ran up large accounts with trades people, and she feared those poor tradespersons did not always get paid for the services they rendered. Sadly, many figures of Society thought their patronage was payment enough for all the costly fabrics and skilled needlewomen's and tailors' time. Thankfully, her father would never be that kind of client.

"We will work around the clock to have the first gown to your lovely daughter by tomorrow afternoon," Mrs. Gainsworth said.

Unaccountably, Dot had found herself, with each dress, wondering if Lord Appleton would think her attractive in it. More and more, she thought about him and wondered if it was truly possible that he could be attracted to her.

She most certainly was attracted to him.

By the time they made the rounds of all the other trades people whose skills would contrive to render Dot fashionable, they were too exhausted to go to the Pump Room.

"Are you certain you won't receive callers until your new finery arrives?" Miss Appleton asked her.

"I'm certain, but it looks as if Mrs. Gainsworth will oblige us with the first dress late tomorrow."

Miss Appleton nodded. "Your father's terribly clever. He knows how to expedite matters. As soon as Mrs. Gainsworth learned she'd get paid by the piece upon delivery, she determined to work around the clock! You are most fortunate to have a father with such deep pockets."

"To be truthful, I don't think about Papa's fortune. Having a wealthy father never seemed important back at Blandings."

An uncharacteristic solemnity edged into Miss Appleton's normally cheerful voice. "Unfortunately, in the rest of the world, wealth is important." Then she attempted to brighten, but Dot could tell something must be troubling her friend. "Expect my brother and me to call on you Thursday."

Just knowing she would see Lord Appleton again lightened her step. Dot said good-bye to Miss Appleton in front of the glovemaker's shop on Milsom Street, and they each walked in different directions to return to their homes.

As soon as the Pankhursts reached their home, Mr. Pankhurst put a hand to his head and spoke in a feeble voice. "I do believe I've overtaxed myself today. I must take to my bed." Dot felt dreadfully guilty that she was responsible for her father's discomfort. Her brows lowered with concern, and she spoke in a tender voice. "Shall I have Cook send up a tray? Or have you completely lost your appetite?" When Dot felt poorly, she could never eat.

"I shall have to force myself to eat. One in my condition must keep up his strength." Her father—whose slightly portly physique gave testament to his always hearty appetite—turned and began to mount the stairway, groaning with each step. "I may have to procure a sedan chair and have two strong footmen hoist me up the stairs in it."

"Or we could put your bed in the saloon."

"Never! I must have the privacy my bedchamber affords." His voice had suddenly increased in stridency.

Dot wasted no time in getting down on the Turkey carpet in the drawing room and playing with her kitties. "Did you miss me today?" It wasn't often she was away from them for this many hours.

Of the four, only Nellie came to climb upon her, her purr vibrating as she came to settle on Dot's lap. As happy as Dot was to see them, she felt as if something were missing. Her thoughts kept wandering to Lord Appleton. Everywhere they had gone that day, she had looked for him. Being with Miss Appleton without her brother was rather like going about with only a single glove or a solo shoe. She felt his absence acutely. How could it be that after just one day's acquaintance she had become so attached to him?

Would he approve of her new dresses? More importantly, would he find her attractive in them? She thought of the indecent waltz she had witnessed the previous night. Her face flamed when she thought of waltzing with Lord Appleton, yet she could not deny she longed to find herself waltzing in his arms in her new green silk dress.

She wondered which dress Mrs. Gainsworth would deliver tomorrow afternoon. Dot was impatient for Thursday to come. She grew impatient to see his lordship. Would his attentions to her still be as marked as they had been the previous day?

* * *

When Appleton and his sister arrived at the

Pankhurst residence, he was astonished at the number of servants required for this family of two. Astonished and somewhat intimidated. Two towering footmen had met them at the door. How in the devil had Pankhurst found two specimens of exactly the same size? And rather an impressive size it was!

As Appleton stood in the gracefully appointed marble entry hall with its curving staircase, a third servant—an austere butler—went to announce him and his sister to their master. Appleton understood what it must feel like to be the runt of a litter, though he was a bit above average height himself.

To give Pankhurst his due, the man did not give off airs as did many vastly wealthy men. He personally came to greet them in a most agreeable manner. "So good of you to call, my lord. Do come into the drawing room. My Dot will be down momentarily. Wait until you see her in her new finery! Don't mind if I say so myself. She's a beauty!"

He led them into an elegant chamber, furnished in high quality French furnishings and painted a sunny yellow. "Indeed she is," Appleton agreed as he took a seat on a silken sofa in the same bright yellow.

How fortunate Appleton was to have discovered the Pankhurst wealth before the rest of Bath had the opportunity to swoop down on the unmarried lady like vultures. It was only a matter of time before the rest of the city learned of her father's vast fortune.

According to his sister, no expense had been spared the previous day in making Miss Pankhurst into the finest dressed lady in all of

Bath. All the city's shopkeepers would be spreading the word about the new heiress in town.

It was imperative that he secure her affections before the onslaught.

Miss Pankhurst then entered the chamber wearing a snowy muslin dress sprigged with tiny purple flowers. He deemed it most fashionable, but it was her figure with its meaty bits that was even more to his liking. What had happened to the old Miss Pankhurst? This young woman really was lovely. Even that mahogany-coloured hair of hers was elegantly styled.

He then noticed a parade of cats following her into the room.

"Miss Pankhurst!" Annie exclaimed. "You are provokingly beautiful. You've procured a maid to style your hair. Such envy-worthy loveliness!"

Dot patted her coif. "Thank you. I'm so pleased."

"Pray tell, how *did* you find her?" Annie asked.

"I asked our exceptionally competent housekeeper, and before I knew it, she had this wonderful girl here. Did she not do herself credit?"

"Indeed she did," Annie said. "She's astonishingly talented."

"I thought so, too." Miss Pankhurst then did a most unladylike thing. She plopped on the rug and began to play with her cats. There were four of them altogether.

Appleton was gratified that Elvin had not accompanied him and his sister this day. If he had, there would be no end to the teasing Appleton would have to endure over that lady's obsession with her demmed cats.

One of those cats—quite a fat one the colour of

marmalade—strayed from the others and had the audacity to come and rub its furry self against Appleton's leg. He prayed Miss Pankhurst would not notice if he gave it a slight kick in an attempt to dislodge the insistent feline from his calf. But the beast still did not budge.

When it began to move a moment later, he thought perhaps it was a delayed reaction to his miniscule kick, but his hopes were dashed when the orange cat came to settle its bottom on his boots, the very ones that Digby had polished to a mirror-like shine that very morning. The blasted cat purred so loudly Appleton was certain its owner several feet away could hear the annoying sound.

She then turned her smiling face to him. "Oh, do look! Lover Boy loves Lord Appleton."

"Smartest cat in the bunch," Mr. Pankhurst said. "Of course, he's the only male. He instinctively knows when males enter our domain."

"I think, Papa, you're being very obtuse. Each of my kitties is highly intelligent."

It was all Appleton could do not to contradict the lady. Cats were such inferior creatures when compared to dogs. Did not everyone know it was dogs who were highly intelligent? As besotted as Miss Pankhurst was over these feather-brained felines, even she, he would vow, would be powerless to teach them a single skill.

The lady's attention returned to him. "You must have a special way with cats, my lord."

She need not know of his dislike of cats. "I confess I've hardly ever been around them."

Her face collapsed. "What a very great misfortune." Then she brightened. "But Lover Boy will ensure that that changes. He obviously adores you."

Lover Boy? That was the silliest name he'd ever heard. No one would ever saddle a dog with a ridiculous name like that. "I presume you gave your cat such a . . . an affectionate name because of his overly friendly nature?"

"Oh, yes. Just listen to him purr. Is he not a darling? Don't you just want to cuddle with him?"

Annie started giggling. "I don't believe my brother thinks in such terms, Miss Pankhurst, but I completely understand. Would that I had *one* kitten of my own, and you are fortunate to possess four! I should think I'd been transported to heaven."

He hated like the devil that Annie was encouraging her!

"But you're blessed with siblings," Miss Pankhurst countered. "I had none." Her brows lowered. "Why is it you cannot have at least *one* kitten of your own?"

"It's our youngest sister, Abby," Appleton said. "She cannot tolerate being in the same chamber with cats."

Annie nodded. "Her eyes water like a spigot, and she sneezes uncontrollably."

Miss Pankhurst looked stricken. "How immensely unfortunate. I should die if such a calamity befell me." Her lips screwed up as if she were deep in thought. "Did you not just say your youngest sister is named Abby?"

"Yes."

"Do all the girls possess names starting with the letter *A*?"

"Indeed they do," he said. "A very astute observation on your part." Once again, he counted himself fortunate she wasn't the dimwit they'd expected.

"Thank you, my lord," Miss Pankhurst acknowledged. "But the use of *A* names is not a practice, I take it, your family used with the sons?"

He shook his head. "While our parents fancied alliterative names, the Appleton males have always reused the same family names."

Miss Pankhurst nodded. "So there's Annie and Abby . . . What are the other sisters' names?"

"There's just one other. She's Agnes," Annie answered, petting a black and white cat. "And what's this little one's name?"

"Nellie."

"You must share the evolution of Nellie's name," Mr. Pankhurst said from his big chair near the fire. He was powerless to stifle a chuckle.

With no more encouragement than that, Miss Pankhurst scooped up the cat, kissed it on its whiskered cheek—did cats have cheeks?—and proceeded to show the visitors that the fur around the animal's right eye made an almost perfect black circle. "You see the patch around Nellie's right eye?"

He and Annie nodded.

"Well, because of that, I named this kitty Lord Nelson."

"Oh, yes," Annie said. "Because that looks exactly like an eye patch."

"It does." Miss Pankhurst shrugged. "However, before Lord Nelson was a year old, it became clear to us *he* was a *she* when she presented us with a litter of kittens." She shrugged. "Thus Lord Nelson became Nellie."

Appleton couldn't help himself. He chuckled.

Loudly.

Miss Pankhurst readily joined in the laughter.

"What if your *Lover Boy* had turned out to be a lady?" he asked. "What might you have named him, er, her, then?"

"I suppose something like Sweetie Girl."

The butler entered the chamber, cleared his throat, and said, "A Mrs. Moreland and two Mrs. Blankenships to see you, Miss Pankhurst."

"Have them come here." Miss Pankhurst's gaze flicked to Annie. "Two Mrs. Blankenships?"

Annie shrugged. "There are actually three residing in Bath at present. I daresay Glee's come with her sister-in-law Mary Blankenship, who's married to Jonathan Blankenship."

"Jonathan Blankenship's the very best of friends with my friend Sir Elvin's twin brother, who's a scholar of some repute."

"As is Jonathan Blankenship," Annie added.

Miss Pankhurst's natural smile deepened even more. "Two scholars?"

Appleton nodded.

"You say it's Sir Elvin's twin who is the scholar?"

Appleton laughed out loud. No one who knew Elvin would ever take him for a scholar. "Definitely his twin," he finally said,

Miss Pankhurst's mouth lifted to a smile, and her black eyes shone with delight. "How exciting. I do hope I will have the privilege of meeting these great minds."

"It will be my honor to introduce you," he said.

"I declare," Mr. Pankhurst said, "I should be honored to meet them also."

"Consider it done."

Those very large, very dark eyes of Miss

Pankhurst's met Appleton's. "I didn't know Sir Elvin had a twin brother. Are they identical?"

He nodded. "I've known them almost all of my life, and I still can't tell one from the other, at least visually. When they speak, I know which one's intelligent about classical learning—and which one knows more about wom. . ." Appleton stopped himself. He couldn't allow Miss Pankhurst to know his best friend was knowledgeable about women and mistresses and gambling and sporting pursuits. That wouldn't do at all. He cleared his throat. "About horses."

"My Dot will be in her element with those brilliant men," Mr. Pankhurst said. "You will never find a more clever female."

"Papa! I beg you to cease praising me. It's most mortifying."

Mr. Pankhurst shrugged. "I shall try, but it's difficult. I only speak the truth."

"Stop!"

It wasn't Jonathan's wife who accompanied Pixie into the chamber. It was Jonathan's mother.

After the introductions were made, Glee Blankenship flung herself on the Turkey carpet in order to play with the cats. What was it about these stealthy creatures that so excited those of the opposite gender? Perhaps Sir Elvin should have come. They might be on to something here. The way to a lady's heart might be through her cat.

Appleton reached down to pet Lover Boy. He might feign affection for the beast, but he would draw the line at calling it by that ridiculous name.

"I can just see Little Gregory with a kitten of his own," the elder Mrs. Blankenship said, smiling at her daughter-in-law.

Glee's eyes narrowed. "Pray, Mama, you must curb your partiality for our son. I'm sure Joy would enjoy a kitty just as much as her brother."

"Forgive me. You know how much I adore Joy even if she is more rambunctious than half a dozen unruly lads! It's just that little boys have always held the key to my heart."

Glee rolled her eyes. "I will own, Little Gregory is possessed of the sweetest nature imaginable. He's very easy to spoil." She eyed her hostess. "I would love to own cats. Unfortunately, my husband does not share my enthusiasm. Perhaps one day you'd allow me to bring my children to play with these little fellows."

Appleton and Blanks had another thing in common: a dislike of felines.

"I should be thrilled. But only one of my kitties is actually a fellow," Miss Pankhurst answered.

Appleton stopped himself from thinking about playing a jest on Blanks. He'd always been a great lover of practical jokes, but he must conduct himself with more maturity now that he was thirty and head of the house. Therefore, he decided not to encourage Miss Pankhurst to trot through Bath with her bevy of cats or take them to the Blankenships' house on Queen Square.

Besides, if he were going to ask for the young woman's hand in marriage, he'd as lief she not make herself a laughingstock by parading about the city with her cats.

"So, Mrs. Blankenship," Miss Pankhurst said to Glee, "you have a son and a daughter?"

Glee's pretty face brightened. "Indeed we do."

"And those are your only grandchildren?" Mr. Pankhurst asked the elder Mrs. Blankenship.

"Yes. My son Jonathan has not been married

long, and there are just the two Blankenship sons."

"You are indeed blessed," Mr. Pankhurst said to the elder lady. "Two sons and two grandchildren."

The woman's lashes lowered coyly at being addressed by a man of her own age. Had the elder woman learned of Mr. Pankhurst's vast wealth? Was the widow hoping to snag another wealthy husband? "Indeed I am, Mr. Pankhurst. I do wish you could see my little darlings."

"You must bring them to see my daughter's cats."

"Depend upon it." Appleton stood. "I must be off." His gaze went to Miss Pankhurst, who stood and faced him. "Will you allow me to collect you this afternoon for a visit to the Pump Room?" he asked.

She looked to her father, who almost imperceptivity nodded.

"Will Miss Appleton come, too?" Miss Pankhurst asked.

"Yes, of course."

Chapter 5

After all their guests had departed, her papa acted like the barnyard rooster who'd turned into a peacock. "I declare, Dot, that lord means to court you! Can you credit it? The daughter of Westmoreland Pankhurst, country squire, Lady Appleton!" He quite forgot his gouty foot as he began to waltz about the drawing room, a smile stretching across his face.

The very notion that Lord Appleton would bestow his affections upon her stole Dot's breath away and caused a rumbling to her insides. She dared not allow herself to contemplate a match that was so improbable—and so unequal. No peer of the realm would be interested in the exceedingly unfashionable Miss Dorothea Pankhurst who had never before traveled beyond the borders of rural Lincolnshire. "No, Papa, I cannot credit it. The man is merely being agreeable."

"I beg to differ. He's possessed of very discerning taste. One has only to look at him to know what a keen eye he has. That trained eye enabled him to detect your beauty beneath what I've come to understand was hideously outdated clothing."

"But I am not beautiful. It's only because you are so partial to me that you find me possessed of such qualities."

He shook his head emphatically. "Even Miss Appleton agrees that you are quite lovely."

"Then she's even kinder than her brother."

"You exasperate me! It's as plain as the nose on my face that Lord Appleton is besotted over my daughter."

"You, my dear father, are blinded by your paternal partiality." Then a terrifying thought occurred to her. What if Lord Appleton was only feigning attraction to her in order to get his hands on her dowry?

Having lived all her life away from Society, Dot had never had to concern herself with fortune hunters. Even in Bath, the prospect of attracting such mercenary men had never entered her mind. Truth to tell, she had not even considered that she'd meet *any* men at all. She'd come here in the singular hope of restoring her father's health.

Then she had met Lord Appleton and been dazzled by everything about him: his good looks, his amiable ways, the tasteful manner in which he dressed, and most of all, his attentions to her.

Was he genuine? He had to be. No one in Bath could have known how exceedingly wealthy her father was. After all, until her shopping foray, they had not flaunted their wealth. God knows, the clothes she had worn when she met Lord Appleton had most thoroughly disguised that the Pankhursts were possessed of a large fortune.

No, she thought to herself, his lordship could not possibly have known of her generous dowry. But she could not account for his interest in her. How she wished she could believe her father was right about the handsome lord being attracted to her.

For, as much as she wished it were not so, she was most decidedly attracted to him.

That did not mean she was foolish enough to envision herself becoming Lady Appleton. She was intelligent enough to know they were from o different worlds, and she did not belong in his.

Even so, she determined that she would look as lovely as she possibly could when he called for her that afternoon.

* * *

Appleton and Annie were just about to leave their house on Camden Crescent when Elvin called. As soon as Appleton got a good look at his friend, he became alarmed. "Is everything all right?"

"I am well, as is my family. I beg a private word with you, though."

Appleton felt as if he'd been struck. Elvin did not look at all well. What the devil was amiss? "Come to the library."

After closing that chamber's door behind them, he whirled to his friend. "What's wrong?"

"You remember Ellie from Mrs. Starr's?"

"Of course." It was barely a week earlier that young lady was present at his ruination.

"She's been murdered."

Appleton's eyes widened. His gut clenched. "How?"

"Her body was found floating in the River Avon. It is believed she was strangled to death."

Sickened, Appleton collapsed onto a chair. He pictured her youthful prettiness, her flashing blue eyes, her tinkling laugh. It seemed incredulous that anyone so lively could be dead. "How did you learn this?"

"It was in the *Bath Chronicle*. It said she didn't

show up for work last night. Poor Mrs. Starr identified her body."

"My God, who would do such a thing?" Appleton shook his head solemnly. "She wasn't much more than a girl."

"I daresay she was younger than Annie, er, Miss Appleton."

Appleton nodded. "The madman must be one of those sex maniacs."

"I daresay you're right."

"I hope the fiend is apprehended."

"Death's too good for him." Elvin shook his head in a most morose fashion. "I believe I could kill him myself. Ellie was such a pretty little thing."

"All of Mrs. Starr's girls are pretty things, old fellow." Sitting here brooding would neither bring her back nor apprehend the man responsible for her death. Appleton stood and sighed. "Care to accompany me and Annie to the Pump Room? We're going to collect Miss Pankhurst."

"Anything to keep my mind off this terrible tragedy."

* * *

As her father sat in an invalid's chair, Miss Pankhurst kissed him on the cheek, and one of those massive footman began to push the older man along the pavement as Lord Appleton approached their house.

"Taking the waters this afternoon, sir?" Appleton asked Mr. Pankhurst as the two came abreast of one another.

"It's the reason I've come to Bath. My daughter assures me they will restore my fragile health." He sighed. "I, on the other hand, fear my infirmities are beyond help."

"I agree with your daughter," Appleton said. "You're still a young man."

Mr. Pankhurst sighed. "Would that you were right."

As the invalid's chair moved along, Appleton turned his attention to the woman he meant to court. How fashionable she looked in her flimsy—though beautiful in its delicacy—white under dress topped by a lavender tunic. Even though the neckline was high, his gaze skimmed appreciatively over the sizable swell of her bosom. "You're looking most fetching, Miss Pankhurst."

She smiled. "It's awfully clever of me to first show myself to disadvantage by presenting myself to Bath Society in rags, is it not?" She gave a little laugh.

Her laugh was contagious. Annie, too, joined in. Appleton found himself nodding. "And I thought your father was boasting about your intelligence when he was merely being truthful."

She looked heavenward. "Pray, pay no attention to my father when I am the topic of his boasts. Parents are no accurate judge of their offspring."

Annie hooked her arm through Miss Pankhurst's as the four of them started toward the Pump Room. "Well spoken, Miss Pankhurst—not that I disagree with your dear father. My father was so blinded by his affection for his daughters, he was in want of sense. In his eyes, we were each perfection. And, I must say, at times he embarrassed us excessively."

"Especially when he insisted Abby could sing like a nightingale," Appleton said, chuckling.

Laughing, Annie nodded. "When her voice is, unfortunately, excruciatingly offensive."

He needed a chuckle. The news of Ellie's

murder preyed on him. He could not purge from his mind the horrifying thought of her frail, lifeless body floating in the river. Why would anyone do such a thing?

When they arrived at the Pump Room, Glee Blankenship was already there, but this time she was accompanied by the younger Mrs. Blankenship, who had married Blanks' half-brother Jonathan. Appleton's group joined the two ladies.

"I declare, Blanks almost didn't allow me to come," Glee said.

Appleton lifted a brow. It wasn't like Blanks to be so authoritarian with his wife. A more indulgent husband Appleton had never seen. "That doesn't sound like Blanks."

Glee sighed. "It's just that he worries so about me. And about our children. You know what a tender heart he possesses."

Appleton nodded. "What has him so worried?"

As soon as he spoke, he knew.

Glee's eyes rounded. "Have you not heard? There's a madman running about Bath murdering young women!"

His stomach fell. The expression on his face turned grim. "Indeed. I had heard."

Elvin nodded. "In fact, we knew the unfortunate victim."

Annie whirled to Elvin, her eyes wide with fear. "How dreadful! Who was she?"

"A young woman employed at Mrs. Starr's Gaming Establishment."

Miss Pankhurst's brows lowered as she faced Glee. "Are you saying there's a homicidal maniac in Bath?"

"Indeed, Miss Pankhurst," Glee confirmed. "It's

really the most horrid thing. The young woman was found murdered in the River Avon this very morning."

Miss Pankhurst looked at Elvin. "This is the woman from Mrs. Starr's?"

He nodded solemnly.

"The poor woman," Miss Pankhurst murmured.

Annie echoed the remark, then questioned Glee. "How did you learn of this wretched crime?"

"It was in the *Bath Chronicle* this afternoon. The edition came out earlier than usual, I suppose because of the sensational news."

"I do hope my father doesn't see the *Chronicle*. I shouldn't want to return to Blandings," Miss Pankhurst said.

Appleton hoped so, too. It wouldn't do at all for the man to whisk his daughter back to Lincolnshire—though he wouldn't blame him if he wished to. Appleton himself didn't at all like to think of Annie being in danger from the maniac. He thanked God his other two sisters were far away and vowed to more strictly guard Annie until the deranged madman was apprehended.

"I think Blanks is right to be worried," he said, eyeing first his sister and then Miss Pankhurst. "In fact, from this point forward, you ladies should not be permitted to be out after dark without the protection of a man." He stood a bit straighter. "I offer myself for that role to both of you."

"And if you're not available," Elvin said, "I shall offer myself." Then he proffered his arm to Annie. "May I escort you about the chamber, Miss Appleton?"

Appleton stepped up to Miss Pankhurst. "May I have the honor, Miss Pankhurst?"

She placed her hand on his arm. He'd not

noticed before that her hands were dainty. As they walked, he kept thinking about poor Ellie, which put him in a foul mood. He was not fit company for anyone, much less a lady he meant to woo.

What if Mr. Pankhurst, upon hearing there was a madman killing young women in Bath, promptly removed his precious daughter from this city?

She was Appleton's only hope of redeeming the family fortunes—and saving Annie from a reprobate like Henry Wolf.

Even though he'd only known the lady a few days, perhaps Appleton needed to declare himself to Miss Pankhurst now. The very thought of shackling himself frightened him. That and regret that he would not be marrying for love. Nevertheless, he must act. For his family.

Now, to get up the courage. . .

She softly stroked his hand. "I'm very sorry, my lord, that you've lost your friend. I can tell that you're greatly saddened over the death of the young lady from Mrs. Starr's." Her voice was gentle and kind.

How many other young women from the upper middle classes would be so sympathetic over the loss of what many would consider an insignificant lower-class girl employed at a gaming establishment?

"Tell me about her."

For some unaccountable reason, he found he *did* want to discuss Ellie. "She wasn't very old. How old are you, Miss Pankhurst?"

She swallowed. "Three-and-twenty."

Was she embarrassed to admit she was still unwed at such an age? "I would say that Ellie—I don't know her surname—was younger than you. Perhaps one-and-twenty. She could have been even younger. She was very pretty. Blonde and small boned. Like most girls in her situation, I suspect her life may have been hard before she came to Mrs. Starr's, but she was always cheerful, and I think those girls were happy to have a position where they earned a decent wage—and it didn't hurt that they were admired by the men who were their patrons. Most of the men were from a higher station than these girls would normally mix with."

He took a deep breath and continued. "While some of the girls there were no innocents, no taint ever touched Ellie. She was a good girl. She did not deserve such an end." His voice cracked.

"No one deserves such an end."

He covered her hand with his. "Thank you, Miss Pankhurst."

"For what?"

"For listening. For understanding. For caring about an unfortunate girl few will miss."

Those great eyes of hers glistened. "We must do everything in our power to see that her death is not forgotten, that her murderer does not go free."

He nodded solemnly. Having Miss Pankhurst as his ally was comforting.

* * *

Dot had been in rather a hurry to get home from the Pump Room. It was her desire to get the *Bath Chronicle* before her father saw it. Were he to read about a madman killing young women, he'd hasten her back to Blandings even before her fine dresses could be delivered.

As frightening as it was to know a murderer lurked in this lovely city, she did not want to return home. Now that she'd been exposed to much more of the world and met and mingled with interesting people near her own age, life in Lincolnshire would be unbearably restrictive.

And, more than anything, she was not ready to terminate this fledgling relationship with Lord Appleton. Why was it when she wasn't with him, she longed to be with him? Why was it that being with him brought her so much joy? She did not understand why this man affected her so profoundly, but she couldn't bear the thought of never seeing him again.

As soon as she entered their home that afternoon, Dot snatched up the *Chronicle* from the entry hall's long sideboard and raced to the library to read about the demise of the unfortunate Ellie. It only took a moment to read the account:

The pristine waters of our city's River Avon were the scene of a most grisly occurrence on this morning of November eleventh when the lifeless body of a young woman was discovered. Jeremiah Biggs alerted magistrates to the unfortunate tragedy this morning whilst he was powering his boat downstream.

The body was identified as Miss Ellie Macintosh by Mrs. Isobel Starr, proprietor of a gaming establishment on Dorchester Street. According to Mrs. Starr, she became alarmed when Miss Macintosh did not show up for work last night and called at her lodgings, only to discover the young woman was not there, either.

It was thought Miss Macintosh was twenty years of age and had been in the employment of Mrs. Starr for the past three years. "She never missed a day, so I feared something was amiss," Mrs. Starr told the magistrates. She went on to say that Miss Macintosh had no known enemies and was very well liked.

This leaves magistrates to believe the death may be a crime of passion, perhaps even have been perpetrated by a sex maniac. Until the murderer is apprehended and brought to justice, all young women are advised to exercise caution whilst moving about the city, especially at night.

Dot folded up the paper, went to her bedchamber, and hid it in a drawer. *Papa must never see this.*

But Mr. Pankhurst did not have to see the newspaper accounting. When he returned from taking the baths, he immediately summoned his daughter.

"There's been a hideously brutal murder, and I wish us to return to Blandings immediately," he told her.

Chapter 6

Dot was taken aback by the panic in her father's voice. She'd never seen him appear so vulnerable. She was at once touched because he feared losing her, and she was shocked that he'd quickly abandoned his invalid's chair to storm about the library, ranting about the lunatic who was threatening young women. He was so distraught he'd forgotten about his own infirmities.

For herself, Dot would risk facing the madman to stay in Bath. She must find a way to convey to her father how important it was that she be allowed to remain here.

Then, like the swipe of a hand across a frosted window, she clearly saw what she could say to change his mind. She recalled how proud he'd been that morning when he'd said, *My daughter, Lady Appleton.* She didn't for a moment believe she was fit to be Lord Appleton's wife, nor did she believe he would ask her to be, but for now, her father must believe such a declaration was imminent.

"Papa! I beg that you sit down so we can discuss the matter. You'll only aggravate your gout."

He came to sit on his favorite chair near the fire, and Dot bent over to pull up a stool upon which he could rest his foot. Then she sat facing him upon the velvet sofa the same shade of royal blue as the room's damask walls. "I am not going to leave Bath."

"You will do what I tell you to do, young lady!" His voice had risen again.

She shrugged and sighed. "You shall ruin all my prospects. I thought you desired that I wed. Just this morning you told the elder Mrs. Blankenship how fortunate she was to have two grandchildren, and that you longed to have grandchildren. And now you're spoiling my chances to find a husband." She pouted.

Next, she expertly extracted her trump. "I thought you had noticed how partial Lord Appleton is to me. . ."

Her father's brows shot up, and a smile tweaked at the corners of his mouth. "I most decidedly have noticed! Has he said anything?"

She shrugged again. "Little things here and there. As you know, I'm ignorant of courting, but I believe his efforts to gain my favor must be for the purpose of asking for my hand."

"Well, that paints a very different picture. I wouldn't worry so about you as long as there was a man to take care of you, to protect you, to love you."

Her stomach—or was it her heart?—did an odd flutter when he said *to love you*. "As a matter of fact, my dearest Papa, that's exactly what his lordship pledged to do this afternoon."

Her father's face went from gloomy to elated. "That sounds like a declaration to me."

She nodded. "He made his vow whilst a group of us were discussing the murder. He said he would not allow either me or his sister to move about this city without his protection." She hadn't even had to lie to her father to make her case.

A huge smile lifted her father's face. "See! I was right. The man's besotted over you." He looked at her with shimmering eyes. "Lord Appleton *is* possessed of very fine taste in everything—especially in young women."

As they spoke, the raindrops began to spray upon the windows. They would not be leaving their home for the rest of the day. When would she see Lord Appleton again?

* * *

Appleton sat at the desk in his library, rain thumping against the windows, gray skies contributing to his forlorn mood that had been mounting all day.

The door squeaked open and Annie poked her head in. Her brows lowered as she regarded him with a quizzing look. "Bertram said you wished to see me?"

He stood. "Yes, please come. Let's sit by the fire. It's certainly turned much colder."

She pulled her scarlet shawl about her shoulders. He would never understand women's fashions. Why in the devil did style dictate the exposure of delicate female skin when it was cold enough to tint that skin purple?

"Indeed," she said.

They sat together on the sofa that faced the hearth. Save for his bed, this was the coziest place in the house. That's why he'd selected it for this conversation with his sister.

Asking her to join him in the library was most irregular, but owing to the closeness the two had always shared, this meeting was necessary.

He drew a deep breath. "I wanted to tell you I'm

going to offer for Miss Pankhurst."

Annie gasped.

"You don't approve?" he asked.

Her eyes met his, scrutinizing him as if he were a stranger. He kept waiting for her to speak. "I approve of Miss Pankhurst very much," she finally said. "She's intelligent, refreshingly honest, and she is possessed of a kind heart. The man who marries her will be most fortunate—and not just in material wealth."

Her gaze went to the flickering flames, and her voice lowered. "What I don't approve of is that you don't love her. She deserves to wed a man who will love her and cherish her. And that man is not you." She turned back to him, her eyes as cold as her voice. "I don't want to see her hurt."

He swallowed. "Nor do I. I won't lie to you and claim that I'm in love with Miss Pankhurst, but I do admire her, and I would never hurt her."

Annie did not respond for a moment. "You and I have never spoken on such matters before, but I've long known about your Mrs. Pratt."

His stomach plummeted. He hated like the devil that his sisters knew of his mistress. This was not a matter he wished to discuss with Annie. So he stayed silent.

"Having a mistress would hurt Dorothea Pankhurst. She's the kind of young lady who, when she consents to marry, will love a man with all her heart and would never understand a husband who wanted to share his bed with another woman. It would destroy her."

He swallowed again. "But a great many married men keep mistresses."

"I'm well aware that our father did, but I would never wish to marry a man who behaved as did our father. It's wrong."

He bowed his head. "I know."

"Miss Pankhurst, tender-hearted creature that she is, would never be able to tolerate an unfaithful husband. She's never known anything but total love. You've seen how her father dotes on her. And look at her and those adorable cats! She only understands love. She would know it and be deeply hurt if she discovered you didn't love her."

Of course, his sister was right. The last thing he wanted was to hurt Miss Pankhurst. It would be crueler than kicking one of his trusting and loyal hounds. "What if I agreed to dismiss Mrs. Pratt? Then would you look more favorably upon my union with Miss Pankhurst?"

He hadn't even seen his mistress since before that fateful night he lost his fortune at Mrs. Starr's. He'd known he was going to have to dismiss her because he simply had no funds to keep her.

Strangely, the prospect of parting ways with her did not disturb him. He only hoped she would quickly find another generous protector to replace him.

"I would." Annie turned once again to gaze into his eyes, so much like her own. "I don't fully understand why you're so compelled to offer for a woman with whom you are clearly *not* in love, but since you are, you must agree to make every effort to fall in love with the woman you want to make your wife."

What a foolish thing his sister was trying to mandate! One simply couldn't will oneself to fall in love. However, he did owe it to Miss Pankhurst, if she did him the goodness of consenting to become his wife, to try to be a loving, faithful husband.

Like Annie, he had not approved of his father's infidelities. It wasn't fair to the lovely woman who'd been their mother—and a devoted wife. He vowed to be a better husband.

If he had the opportunity.

His chest tightened. If only he loved Miss Pankhurst at the outset. How much simpler things would be. Simpler and more enjoyable. Far more enjoyable.

* * *

Between the dampness and the unrelenting rain over the next three days, Dot insisted that her father not leave the house. "I don't need you to take lung fever and die on me," she told him.

"And whilst you are housebound, my dear daughter, I shall insist that we take this opportunity to bring in a real dancing master. I'll not have the daughter of Westmoreland Pankhurst being a wallflower at these Bath assemblies."

She could not refuse. She shared her father's wish that she be able to move with ease in the same society with Lord Appleton—not that she expected to win his lordship's affections, of course. But a girl had her pride.

And, besides, she admired Miss Appleton very much and did not want to cause any embarrassment to that lady because of her own deficiencies.

So it was that over the next three days her father was able to obtain the services of one Mr. Gibby, who was said to be the most sought-after dance master in Bath. Owing to the man's girth, it was difficult for Dot to imagine he could ever have cut a dashing figure on a dance floor, but she had to concede that it *had* been many years since he had been in the prime of his youth.

When she'd asked her father—who watched each day's proceedings from the comfort of his chair, brandy glass in hand—how old he thought Mr. Gibby was, he'd thought the man might be older than himself.

To his great credit, Mr. Gibby worked tirelessly. When Dot grew winded and begged to rest, the older man carried on with the stamina of a man half his age.

It soon became apparent why the dance master had come so highly recommended, and why he could demand a higher fee than others. He was not only excellent at executing the steps and imparting them to his pupil in a particularly patient manner, but he was also knowledgeable about dances deemed appropriate for a young lady to learn.

Dot became acquainted with the quadrille and the cotillion, which she tended to get mixed up. They practiced longway dancing, and he taught her the old English favorite Sir Roger de Coverley—of which she had been ignorant.

"I have failed my fatherly duties," Mr. Pankhurst lamented. "My daughter's never heard of the Sir Roger. I remember well from the days of my youth when we closed out every assembly with the Sir Roger."

During those three rainy days, her father would not permit her to gallivant about the city. In addition to her dance lessons, she had two other distractions to prevent her from going mad with boredom: reading speculations in the *Bath Chronicle* about Ellie Macintosh's murder and the excitement of daily deliveries of her new wardrobe. One day, two dresses came.

Though the murder continued to occupy the top news spot in each day's *Chronicle,* the murderer had not been apprehended, and virtually no new information had been uncovered.

On the third day, when Topham announced that Lord Appleton was calling, she felt like a butterfly released from a jar.

She and her kitties were on the floor of the drawing room when she looked up to see his lordship stroll into the chamber. All by himself.

Her breath felt trapped in her chest. She didn't know when he'd ever looked better. He had already divested himself, no doubt, of a dripping coat, and stood before her in a jacket the same bark colour as his fashionably styled hair. He paired it with buff breeches and chocolate-coloured boots—all set off with a starchy ivory cravat his valet must have labored over for a considerable period of time. His appearance was sheer perfection.

She couldn't quit staring at him. He was not an exceptionally big man, but he emanated a remarkable strength. This was a man capable of protecting the women in his life.

How she longed to be such a woman.

Since her father had taken to his bed, she instinctively knew she should not be permitted to entertain a single gentleman caller all by herself without benefit of a chaperone. All she could think to say was, "Where is Miss Appleton?"

"I thought it best not to expose the fairer gender to such miserable weather." He cleared his throat. Why did he look so nervous? "And, I wished to speak to you today on a private matter."

She'd been petting Fur Blossom, who curled up purring loudly on her lap. With Lord Appleton's statement, Dot flung away her cat and leapt to her feet. Dare she hope her father's prophesy was coming true? Could Lord Appleton really be seeking her hand in marriage? Her heartbeat drummed.

"Do come, let's stand by the fire," she said. "It's beastly cold today. I can tell from the red in your cheeks that you're cold, my lord."

Surely nothing immoral could occur between two people standing in front of the hearth.

"I pray you did not get out in this dreary weather merely to call upon me, my lord."

"Indeed I did, Miss Pankhurst."

They stood silently, the only noise the hiss of the fire on the grate.

"It's been such an awful week," he finally said. His brows lowered as he looked downward, his leg twitching.

She followed the movement and saw that Lover Boy was rubbing himself on his lordship's leg, back and forth like a saw.

Because of the gravity of the topic they were discussing, she chose to ignore her kitty's actions. "Yes, it has. And I didn't even know Miss Macintosh."

He gave her a wondering gaze. "It's remarkable how well you've come to know me. I *have* dwelt on Miss Macintosh's murder."

"Me, too. It's a ghastly business."

"It's a wonder your father has permitted you to continue in Bath."

She wouldn't lie to him. Precisely. "I've hidden all the newspapers from him."
"Does that mean you're in favor of staying in Bath even though your life could be at risk from that madman?"

"It means I wish to stay in Bath, but have you forgotten, my lord, that you vowed to protect me from the wicked man?" She was so nervous she feared her voice was trembling, like the rest of her.

He chuckled. "So I did."

"It's a pity no one has discovered anything that will lead to the beast's apprehension. I've a mind to make inquiries myself." She looked up at him. "Together with you, of course."

"Do you think because Ellie was just a hostess in a gaming establishment with no family to speak of, no one cares?" he asked.

"I think that could be a sad reality. Were she a duke's daughter, I daresay everyone within a thirty-mile radius of Bath would be questioned, and everyone would be searching for the killer."

He nodded. "You're probably right."

She placed her hand on his forearm. "Do let us make some inquiries. After the rain ceases."

He turned to her and smiled, then placed his hand over hers. He made no effort to remove it.

He also made no effort to speak.

Perhaps she needed to help him. "What is the private matter that brought you here today?"

He let out a sigh. "It may have come to your attention that I prefer spending my time with you more than with any other young woman."

"Yes. A most perplexing choice, I must say. I wondered about that. I can't imagine why you would single me out. Surely there are other women in Bath more worthy of your attentions."

He shook his head. "Oh, not at all, Miss Pankhurst. You are a most singular young woman."

She was happy that he hadn't praised her

beauty which she would have known to be unmerited. But *singular* she did know herself to be.

"And," he continued, "I have exceedingly enjoyed every moment I've been in your company."

"And I yours, my lord."

He cleared his throat again. "I have found in you much to admire, and it would be my greatest wish and a very great honor if you would do me the goodness of consenting to become my wife."

Chapter 7

Ever since she'd seen him standing there in her drawing room, Dot had known why he'd come alone today. Still, she was completely unprepared for the magnitude of his proposal. Its impact was as powerful as a visit from the departed Ellie Macintosh would have been.

How could being *singular* outweigh beauty and pedigree? That must indicate Lord Appleton himself was a most singular man.

Then it occurred to her that somehow, he must have learned of and have need of her fortune. Such knowledge stung.

But she was not about to deny herself this chance at happiness because of potentially bruised pride. For now that she'd met Lord Appleton, she knew no other man would ever appeal.

It wasn't as if she knew him that well. Yet she intrinsically *did* know him. When he'd spoken with such compassion of the unfortunate Ellie Macintosh, she had come to know all she needed to know about the purity of his heart. He was more than a caring brother to Annie. He was a caring person.

And that was all she needed to know. He would be a fine husband—even to an unsophisticated daughter of a wealthy country squire.

It had not escaped her notice that he had not mentioned the word *love*. Though she was well aware that he did not love her now, she believed that because he was a good man, his duty as a husband would compel him to fall in love with the woman to whom he plighted his life.

This wasn't how she had always envisioned a proposal of marriage. It was not a sunny day. They were not surrounded by lush trees or blooming flowers. The man proposing to her was not on bended knee. They were not even facing each other. They stood like two lifeless statues facing the fireplace. No hands were clasped.

And, of course, he was not in love with her.

She turned to him. "It will be my honor to become your wife."

He peered into her eyes with great intensity. Then he took her hands in his and bent to press his lips to them. "You've made me very happy."

He squirmed a bit, and she looked down to see Lover Boy vigorously rubbing the length of his body against Lord Appleton's leg. "Is my kitty bothering you?"

He hesitated a moment, then shook his head. "No, not at all." That slight hesitation indicated her betrothed might not be speaking with complete honesty, but she credited him with doing his best to be tolerant of what mattered to her.

She thought to tease him. "Would you like to pick up Lover Boy for a kitty cuddle?"

He hesitated again. "I'd best not. My man would not be happy were I to return with orange cat hair over my coat."

She nodded. "May I ask you a question, my lord?"

He did not respond for a moment. Did he fear she was going to ask how much he *really* liked cats? Or worse—did he fear she would ask if he was in love with her? "Of course, my love. Anything."

She almost lost her breath when he referred to her as *my love*. She could not credit it. But she vowed to do everything in her power to make him fall in love with her—if it were possible to make one fall in love. "If you're going to be my betrothed, I should wish to call you something less formal than Lord Appleton. What is your Christian name?"

His eyes flashed with mirth. "My given name's Forrester Timothy Appleton, but my friends have always referred to me as Appleton. We are one of the few noble families, like the Spencers and Cowpers, whose title is the same as the family name. That said, members of my family have always referred to me as Timothy. You, my dear, may take your choice."

"Would you mind awfully if I call you Forrester?" She liked the notion of having her own name for him, something no one else used. But certainly not a silly name like she'd give to one of her cats.

He kissed her hand once again and chuckled. "Not at all, love. Now, what shall I call you?"7

"My name's Dorothea, but Papa has always called me. . ."

"Dot. I like it very much. It suits. May I call my future wife Dot?" His gaze dipped to skim her breasts. A tingle coiled through her. For the first time in her life, she felt like a woman. Now she was a woman standing before the man with whom she would become one.

Her heartbeat stampeded. *My future wife.* She felt as if she were a make-believe character in a happy-ending fantasy. "You may."

"I know it would have been more proper of me to ask your father's permission to court you, but I am not a patient man. I couldn't wait another day."

His flattery lifted her even higher than she already felt.

"Can you forgive me?" he asked.

"Of course. You did the right thing."

"Shall I relay the intelligence to your father, or would you like to do so?"

"Allow me to lubricate the way for you. It's essential that my father know this marriage is what I want, or he would never countenance the union. If you care to, you can return here tomorrow to speak to him."

"Then I shall take my leave. I'll call on your father in the morning." He kissed her hand and left.

She wished he would have taken her in his arms and kissed her.

* * *

The drawing open of her silken draperies the following morning awakened Dot. She could tell by how high in the sky the sun was that she had slept late, owing to the fact she had been far too excited the night before to fall asleep.

"My, miss, but you've slept mighty late today," Meg said.

Dot smiled at her maid. It was difficult not to smile at Meg, who was perpetually cheerful. The slender girl with a head of fiery hair was probably five years younger than Dot and, to Dot's great surprise, was thrilled at the prospect of serving *a fine lady* as a maid. Dot could not imagine why anyone would desire a life of servitude, but she vowed to make such a life as pleasant as possible for those who served her.

"It's because I didn't fall asleep until dawn," Dot confessed.

Meg's green eyes brightened. "So you be thinkin' about your young lord what you'll be marrying?"

"Indeed I was."

Still smiling, Meg nodded as she set a tray in front of her mistress and proceeded to pour hot chocolate into a porcelain cup. "I'll be back in a bit to help ye dress, miss."

Throughout the night, Dot had lain in her bed, enclosed within the bed curtains as the fire crackled in her hearth and rain pounded upon her casements, remembering every word that had passed between her and . . . Forrester. She sighed to herself each time she thought of her betrothed by that special name only she would use.

She thought, too, of the sweet words he'd said to her. *My love. . . my dear. . . You've made me very happy.* Not as happy as he'd made her.

And her father.

Papa had been ecstatic when she'd told him of his lordship's proposal, so happy that once again he'd forgotten about his afflictions, flung himself from his sick bed, and begun to dance around his bedchamber. "My daughter, Lady Appleton. Oh, how I wish your dear mother could have lived to see it."

Such a reflection did not make Dot sad because she could not remember her mother at all.

When she finished her chocolate, Meg returned with a freshly pressed dress that Mrs. Gainsworth had just delivered. "Oh, Miss Pankhurst! I never seen anything so beautiful."

Had Dot not been to Bath's elegant Assembly Rooms, she would never have seen a dress as fine as this, either. It was snowy white and embellished with hand-embroidered ivory flowers and trimmed in white lace. She couldn't wait to wear it for Forrester.

"You'll never guess," Meg said, "who's in yer father's library right now."

Dot knew very well who was there. Would her father and her betrothed be discussing marriage settlements and those boring financial matters? How happy she was that she was not taking part in those discussions.

* * *

The prospect of addressing Dot's father made Appleton even more nervous than actually asking the lady for her hand in marriage. He supposed his fears emanated from guilt. Knowing how dearly Mr. Pankhurst cherished his daughter and would expect his daughter to be cherished, Appleton worried that the father would suspect Appleton's true motives for wishing to wed his only child.

What would he say if the father asked him if he was in love with Dot? Appleton abhorred lying.

Mr. Pankhurst put him at ease immediately, clasping his hand and shaking it vigorously as he smiled and referred to him as *my boy*. "Do let's come into my library."

Like the rest of the house, the scarlet library was decorated in excellent taste, with walnut paneled walls and furnishings. "Let us sit on the sofa before the fire. There's quite a chill after all this blasted rain."

They sank into a plush red velvet. "So I'm finally going to have a son," Mr. Pankhurst began. The man could barely contain his glee. He was as excited as a pauper who'd won the sweepstakes. "And a lord at that! I don't mind telling you I couldn't have wished for a better mate for my girl."

"Thank you, sir, but I'm the fortunate one." He hoped such a remark would appease the adoring father.

"You certainly are! Just you wait and see what a fine wife you've selected, my lord. Tell me, when do you plan to marry my girl?"

"I thought we ought to spend a bit of time together to get to know one another better, but I'd like to marry before the month's out. I shall, of course, procure a special license."

Mr. Pankhurst nodded. "A good plan, I daresay. You need to have time with each other without a lot of other people. Just you and Dot, free to talk to each other without disruptions."

"I agree."

The older man cleared his throat. "I've done a bit of asking around about you."

Appleton's stomach dropped. "As a dutiful father should."

"It's come to my attention that you've recently come into some serious financial losses."

Uh oh. He felt as if he'd been walloped with a tree trunk. How in the devil had Pankhurst learned that? Appleton supposed that a man with very deep pockets could obtain whatever information he sought. "I won't deny it. It's the first time in my thirty years I've ever done anything so foolish, and I give you my word it will never happen again."

Mr. Pankhurst's face grew solemn as he

nodded. "I suppose you know I'm a very wealthy man?"

"I won't deny that, either, sir."

"Dot has a generous dowry, and when I'm gone, all my property will go to her."

"You must know that as head of the Appleton family I'm obliged to live on our estate. When not at Bath, I plan to live at Hawthorne Manor as my ancestors have for the past two-hundred-and-fifty years. If Dot should inherit . . . Blandings, is it not?"

"It is."

"It would always stay in our family, but I see it going to one of our children, perhaps a second son. He could even take on the name Pankhurst."

It was a few seconds before the older man responded. Had he offended him? Was something wrong? Then Appleton saw that Mr. Pankhurst must be overcome with emotion. His eyes moistened. "A grandson. A grandson to carry on all I've built. My own father would be so proud."

Appleton had not contemplated having children with Dot, but now the prospect held vast appeal. The more sons, the better! "I should be very proud to enter into a parental partnership with one as . . . as intelligent and as caring as your daughter." He hadn't lied. He truly meant what he said. And he hadn't stretched the truth and professed to be in love with this man's daughter.

"I believe the two of you will have very fine children, and I give you my blessing. My solicitor will draw up the settlements."

The meeting had gone as well as Appleton could have hoped. He rose and shook his future father-in-law's hand. "I'd like to see Dot now, if she's seeing callers."

"She's received another of her lovely dresses, therefore, I believe she'll be wanting to display herself in it to her betrothed." Mr. Pankhurst rang for a servant and when the butler came, instructed him to tell the lady that Lord Appleton was calling on Miss Pankhurst.

"Now," Mr. Pankhurst said, "I'll let you be alone with your betrothed."

Unlike his own sisters, who could take hours to make themselves presentable, his affianced came downstairs almost immediately. He could scarcely credit it when she entered the cozy library. It was as if sparkling sunshine burst into the chamber from beyond the scarlet draperies. It was impossible not to be cheerful when confronted with Dot's perpetual smile.

Miss Dorothea Pankhurst could now hold her own amongst the most fashionable ladies in London's finest ballrooms. Not that she was overly dressed this afternoon. Was his sister responsible for the perfection of Dot's new wardrobe? Although he did not consider himself an expert on female clothing, he believed the simple lines of the dress she wore today not only to be in excellent taste, but the dress was also most becoming.

Its stark white dotted with tiny hand-emroidered flowers complemented her dark colouring. Those very dark locks of hers swept back elegantly as if fashioned by an expert stylist.

He'd not previously noticed how very white her teeth were. He supposed the white of the dress accentuated them.

The more he was discovering about Miss Pankhurst, er, Dot, the more he realized he'd done fairly well for himself. He'd been prepared to sacrifice himself for his family, and while he was still denying himself a true love, he realized the tender-hearted Miss . . . Dot had many fine attributes.

Plus a large fortune.

"I am bereft of words to describe your loveliness, my dear Dot."

She came and offered her hand, and he pressed his lips to it. While he normally only air kissed a woman's hand, this time his lips actually touched her flesh. It was far more intimate than he'd meant.

Colour rose in her cheeks.

"I am gratified the rain has stopped," he said.

"As am I."

They stood motionless.

"I thought perhaps you and I could stroll the city. Now that we are properly betrothed, you won't need the benefit of a chaperone." He proffered his arm.

She moved to him. "I should like that very much."

She went to procure gloves, hat and cape—which he helped to drape around her. Once they were on the pavement, he asked, "Have you been yet to Sydney Gardens?"

"No."

"It's probably not the best day because it will be soggy, but the walk will do us good after this wretched rain that's kept us indoors for so many days."

"The gardens are on the other side of the River Avon, are they not?"

"Yes, but everything's close in Bath. So different than London."

"I would love to see London one day."

"I'll take you there after we're married."

"Do you have a house there?"

He shook his head. "No. Just the one here in Bath and the family seat in Shropshire."

"What is it called?"

"Hawthorne Manor."

"And when you're in London, where do you stay?"

"As close to Westminster as possible. The Appletons have always let houses there for the Parliamentary season."

"You'll serve?"

"I've been putting it off. My brother did and my father before him." He drew a breath. "It's my duty. None of my friends serve. I've been trying to persuade Sir Elvin to stand for the House of Commons. He can afford to."

"Keep trying. He seems to be rather influenced by you."

She was uncommonly perceptive. How could she have known after just a couple of brief meetings how easily Elvin was persuaded by him? "I do feel that if I were in Parliament, Sir Elvin would be more interested in serving."

Cloudy skies and puddled streets kept many indoors but seemed not to have affected the chair men's brisk business. If anything, these burly men were busier than ever on these muddy days. Appleton thought it might be cheaper to use a sedan chair than to repair damage to mud-stained clothing and shoes. Particularly ladies' shoes.

Dot turned to him. "Do you know where Ellie Macintosh lived?"

"I have no idea. Why do you ask?"

"I just thought . . . I thought I'd like to make inquiries about her. It's not right that her killer not be punished."

"I couldn't agree more, but surely you're not suggesting that you plan to try to track down a murdering maniac?"

Her step slowed, and she looked up at him with those big, nearly black eyes. "Not me. *Us*. Did you not vow to be my protector? You said you wouldn't permit me to go about the city without you."

"So I did." Before he'd left his house that morning, he'd warned Annie not to leave. Bath was not a safe place for unescorted young women as long as the madman was loose.

They reached Pulteney Bridge. "The architecture of the buildings on this bridge seems different than the uniformity of architecture throughout the city," she commented. "I do love the designs of the Woods."

She was a remarkably observant young woman. "This bridge was not designed by the Woods. It was designed by the Scottish architect Robert Adam."

"Oh, my sweet heavens, I should have been able to recognize it! Mr. Adam designed the orangery at Blandings for my grandfather, and I've always been interested in his work."

"How fortunate you are. I must tell you Hawthorne Manor has nothing as grand as an orangery nor is it as grand as the least of Adam's designs."

She squeezed his arm. "I'm certain I shall love it."

How strange it seemed that this woman he'd known for so short a time would be mistress of his ancestral home. At least he'd selected someone he admired. Not just any woman could be permitted to step into his dear mother's slippers.

As they continued walking, he grew solemn.

Now that she had brought up Ellie, he was not able to dispel the poor girl from his thoughts. "When you mentioned Ellie Macintosh's lodgings, did you think I might . . . I would never bring this up with you if we were not betrothed . . . did you think I might have been . . . intimate with the young lady?"

She shrugged. "I thought there was some likelihood that she might have been the sort of young woman who mingled with her patrons in such a manner."

"You are right to think that many women employed in such a place conduct themselves in such a way, but Ellie wasn't like that."

"Which makes her death even sadder, does it not?"

"It does. There was an innocence about her."

"We must do something."

"You're right. What do you propose?" He couldn't believe he was asking her for advice. This was a young woman who had admittedly never before been away from rural Lincolnshire. She was seven years his junior. But she was possessed of admirable common sense.

"You must ask Mrs. Starr where Ellie lived. Then we must go there and speak to her landlord and to her neighbors. Someone had to have seen a man milling around. There's a very good probability that man is responsible for her death."

Chapter 8

That night Forrester escorted Dot and his sister to a musical. To make the evening even more enjoyable, Mrs. Gainsworth, who surely must have seamstresses employed around the clock, sent over a pair of extraordinary dresses from which Dot could select this evening's ensemble. She settled on an exquisite dress of crimson crepe with a long-sleeved robe of the same colour, its center opening trimmed entirely in ermine. Dot paired it with ivory satin slippers trimmed in silver.

"Each time I see you, you're more beautiful," Forrester told her when he collected her. She could tell by the sparkle in his mossy eyes he was sincere.

She had never held hands with a man before, so when his fingers laced through hers when handing her into the coach, it caused a significant fluttering in her chest.

Miss Appleton sat across from her in the carriage, and her betrothed came to sit next to her, once more clasping her hand in his. Would she ever grow accustomed to being close to him like this? Would the day ever come when she was so immune to his touch that he no longer elicited a tingling in her nerve endings?

When they arrived at their destination and she

realized how much finer her dress was than Miss Appleton's, she felt wretched. She was much too fond of her future sister to do anything that would put that lady ill at ease.

That afternoon her father had told her the Appletons were not very affluent. Dot vowed that when she and Forrester were married she would take the Appleton sisters to Mrs. Gainsworth's and pay for all their finery.

The very idea of having sisters was almost as thrilling as having their brother for her husband.

To her surprise, the musical was held in the ballroom of the Upper Assembly Room. Forrester had explained that these gracious rooms were often pressed into use for musicals on non-dancing nights.

It was such a windy, cool evening, she was happy to get inside. There, she was pleased to see Glee Blankenship standing at the rear of the half-filled room with an incredibly handsome man. "Is that Mrs. Blankenship's husband?" she whispered to Forrester.

He stared across the chamber. "Yes, that's Blanks. Come, allow me to introduce you."

Dot already thought Glee and her sister, Felicity, were the most beautiful women she had ever beheld, and now she thought Gregory Blankenship, whom, everyone referred to as Blanks, was undoubtedly the most handsome man she had ever seen. He was quite tall—and not just because he was standing beside his wife, who was much smaller than average. In addition, Blanks was possessed of dark eyes and thick, dark hair cut in a fashionable style. Everything about the man's dress bespoke impeccable taste. She recalled having heard that he was in possession of a large fortune—a fortune he had voluntarily shared with his younger half-brother.

"My dear Miss Pankhurst," her betrothed said to her when they reached the handsome couple, "I should like to present to you one of my oldest friends, Gregory Blankenship." Then he looked at his friend. "Blanks, Miss Pankhurst has done me the goodness of consenting to become my wife."

Glee shrieked. Blanks congratulated both of them. Glee threw her arms around Dot. "I am just so very happy for you! I knew when I saw you two together you would be perfect for one another!" Then Glee turned to Forrester. "You've done very well for yourself, Appleton. And it's well past time you settle down."

"Indeed it is, old fellow," Blanks added.

"So all of you men met as young lads at Eton?" Dot asked. She was uncommonly happy with Forrester standing beside her, his hand resting possessively at her waist. He gave every indication of being proud to be her prospective husband. Which made her feel as if her chest had expanded by several inches.

Blanks nodded. "Yes. George, who's Glee's brother as well as the current Viscount Sedgewick; Sir Elvin and his twin; Appleton; and myself. That's five of us"

"Moreland's the only one who's the . . . outsider, so to speak," Forrester said.

Her brows lowered. "Moreland?"

"I don't believe you've met him," Miss Appleton said. "He's married to Mrs. Blankenship's sister."

Dot nodded. "The beautiful blonde."

Each person there said, "Yes," all at once.

"My sister lives just outside of Bath and doesn't always come to events here."

"You will have to see the Morelands' place sometime," Forrester told her. "It's said to be the finest home in all of Somerset."

"I daresay *home* is too modest a word for something as grand as Winston Hall," Miss Appleton said.

Forrester chuckled. "Calling it a palace would be more accurate."

So both beautiful sisters had married very wealthy men, and though the sisters came from an aristocratic family, neither of their husbands were from the nobility. It wasn't uncommon for those with money to marry into pedigree. Isn't that what her own father had wished for her? Forrester was offering his title in exchange for her money—not that she gave a fig for titles. She cared for the man, not the title. She hoped he cared for her, not her fortune.

She prayed there was more to this prospective marriage than a financial agreement. She had allowed herself to believe that Forrester had become her friend and champion before it could possibly have been known in Bath that she was an heiress.

"I hear you talking about this George quite a bit. Is he not in Bath?"

"That's my brother," Glee said. "He prefers his place in the country with his wife and children."

Blanks nodded. "He's certainly sown his fair share of wild oats. In the past."

All at once, she sensed that Forrester stiffened. She looked up at him, and the pleasant expression on his face vanished. His gaze moved to a pasty-faced man who appeared to be making his way toward them.

She watched him watch the man move toward

them. Instead of addressing Forrester, though, the man came to stand beside Miss Appleton. "Good evening, Miss Appleton. How good it is to see you again." Then he looked at her brother and Blanks, nodding to each and giving each of the men a curt address.

It did not escape her notice that both Forrester and Blanks returned his greeting with only a nod. No smile, no words, though both men were, to her observation, normally friendly.

Even the normally congenial Miss Appleton was brusque. "Good evening, Mr. Wolf," was all she had to say to him.

Their group was blocking the center aisle as thickening crowds were moving into the chamber. "We'd best take our seats," Forrester said, presenting his back to Mr. Wolf. How odd, she thought, that he did not even introduce her to this Mr. Wolf.

Obviously, there was some degree of bad blood between Mr. Wolf and Forrester and Blanks.

The Blankenships came to sit on the same row of chairs with them. A gilt harp and a pianoforte stood unattended at the front of the chamber. A few moments after the five of them were seated, she discreetly turned to look about the room. Now it was completely full. On the last row she observed Mr. Wolf sitting by himself. A loner. *I must ask Forrester about this man they all shunned.* Why did they all loathe him so? Even sweet Miss Appleton.

She turned to that lady. "I haven't told you how exceedingly happy I am that we shall be sisters."

Miss Appleton took both her hands. "We couldn't have asked for a better wife for Timothy. I can't wait for our other sisters to meet you. I know they'll love you just as much as I do."

"You will surely turn me into a watering pot, my dearest Miss Appleton."

"You must call me Annie."

"And you must call me Dot."

The entertainers then moved to the front of the chamber, and the voices in the room quieted. A matronly woman in a voluminous gown of flimsy icy blue that one could see through introduced the singer, an exceedingly young and very pretty Miss Elizabeth Milford.

The young lady sang like a nightingale. Dot was mesmerized. Mr. Pankhurst had seen to it that talented pianists and singers instructed Dot, but never had she imagined the human voice could display such perfection as demonstrated by Miss Milford. How could every man in this room not fall in love with the beautiful songstress?

Dot had never felt more inadequate.

The singer was so beautiful it wouldn't have mattered what the lovely young woman wore, but her clothing, too, was perfection. Her crepe dress of the palest green scooped low in front—though the lady's bosom was almost non-existent—and rose to puffs of sleeves. A demi-train of gauze in the same shade of pale green was only barely discernable in the shimmering candlelight. Dot thought she was the most elegant creature she'd ever seen.

Without moving her head, Dot kept looking at Forrester to try to gauge his interest in Miss Milford. He did not remove his eyes from her. Dot found herself wondering if he would have been attracted to the singer were he not betrothed. Would he wish that he had seen her before meeting Dot?

Even though Dot's own dress was lovelier than any in the room, she could not deny that she envied the beautiful Miss Elizabeth Milford.

She was grateful she had come to Bath and been awakened to a world she'd never dreamed existed—even if she still thought of herself as a misfit. Most of all, she was thankful for Forrester. She wasn't foolish enough to believe he was wildly in love with her, but she was hopeful that love would grow between them.

He was a good man. Good men became faithful and loving husbands. As one who had been able to observe village life, Dot had the opportunity to learn a good deal about human nature.

When Miss Milford's performance came to an end, Dot was disappointed. It had been her first-ever musical, and she had not wanted it to stop. Moreover, she did not want this night to be over. Dressing in lovely clothing, being with her new friends, and most of all, being with Forrester was exhilarating. She did not want to go home.

"Excuse me for a moment, love, while I speak to Blanks." Forrester gently set a hand to her arm before moving away.

She then turned to Annie. "How did you enjoy your first musical?" Annie asked.

"It was more wonderful than I ever could have imagined." Her gaze swept to the rear of the chamber, and she saw Mr. Wolf slink away. Lowering her voice, she asked, "Who is Mr. Wolf, and why is everyone so discourteous to him?"

Annie shrugged. "I am not privy to that information. I know only that the man was desirous of meeting me, and my brother rather loathes him. Timothy's disfavor is enough to win my disapproval. I would also add that my brother rarely speaks ill of anyone and is predisposed to like most people. He's an excellent judge of character—and of right and wrong."

Dot smiled. "I am most happy to learn that for I value your opinion most sincerely."

Forrester returned, and to her pleasure, placed his hand to her waist. "Our coach should be waiting."

They said goodnight to the Blankenships and followed the crowd as it emptied from the packed chamber.

A gusty wind accompanied the night's chill. "Good lord, it's beastly cold!" Forrester hurried the ladies toward the waiting carriage.

Once they were in the coach, he addressed his sister. "I've instructed the coachman to drop you off at Camden Crescent."

Annie smirked good naturedly. "So that you and your sweetheart can be alone."

Dot's heartbeat thumped. Would he try to kiss her? How incredibly romantic. Yet at the same time, Dot was terrified her ineptitude would embarrass her. Would he be able to determine she had no experience kissing? Would she do everything wrong? Would she repulse him? She was unable to control her trembling.

He felt it and put his arm around her. "Of course, I want to be alone with my sweetheart."

When the coach pulled in front of Appleton House on Camden Crescent, Dot lifted the velvet curtain to look at it. After all, it was going to be her home. That first day she'd come here she hadn't properly observed it because of her excitement over her new friends and trepidation of trying to learn to dance.

Large brass lanterns flanked the glossy front

door topped by a fan-shaped window.

"Since my brother and Sir Elvin and Blanks are engaged tomorrow, I wondered if you would accompany me to the lending library," Annie asked Dot as she climbed down from the coach, assisted by the coachman.

"That would be lovely."

"I'll come to your house at noon, then," Annie said.

"Our footman will escort you," Forrester said. "It's no longer safe for young women in Bath."

Alone in the coach with Forrester, Dot was comforted that he held her close, but she dreaded the kiss she knew was sure to come—not that she didn't want to kiss him. She did. But she didn't want to suffer what was sure to be his disappointment over her inexperience.

"What are you and the fellows doing tomorrow?" she asked.

"They had wanted to go to a cock fight, but I've sworn off gambling. Forever. So now we're going to spar."

She turned to him. "Spar? I've never heard of that. Is that something men in would do in London at a place like White's? I've heard of White's, you see."

He tossed his head back and laughed. "I don't mean to offend you, my dear, but sparring is most definitely *not* done at a gentleman's club."

"Then it's something one does out of doors?"

"It can be done out of doors, but we generally do it indoors."

Her brows lowered. Her lips pursed in disdain. "Are you going to tell me what sparring is?"

"Sparring, my love, is the act of *practicing* pugilism against a friendly opponent. We do it for fun."

"It sounds dangerous. I do hope you don't get hurt."

"We don't get hurt."

He cleared his throat. "I wanted to be alone with you in order to discuss something I learned this afternoon."

She spun toward him. "You learned something about Ellie Macintosh!"

"I did. I got the direction of her lodgings from Mrs. Starr. I thought perhaps tomorrow afternoon, when we're finished sparring, you and I could make inquiries. You'll probably think of things that a man wouldn't think to ask, things that might be important."

She was pleased that he thought her capable. "I should be honored to accompany you."

The coach then drew up before her house. She waited a moment, expecting him to kiss her. But he didn't. The coachman opened the door, and one of her family's footmen sprang from the house.

"I shall endeavor to meet you tomorrow at the lending library," Forrester said as she moved to exit the carriage. Had he slapped her in the face, she could not have felt more rejected.

He hadn't even wanted to kiss her.

Chapter 9

The two young ladies spent over an hour perusing the shelves of the lending library. During that time they discovered their taste in poetry dovetailed almost perfectly. Though they recognized Lord Byron's genius, his narrative did not speak to either of them. But each confessed that upon reading *Lyrical Ballads*, an exciting new world of poetry had opened up to her. "I declare, Dot," Annie said, "I have memorized almost every stanza penned by Wordsworth."

A huge smile broke over Dot's face. "It's the same with me. In fact, the pages of my copy, which I've brought here to Bath, are pathetically limp and crumpled from use."

"Mine is the same!"

Both women went on to criticize the gothic romances written by Mrs. Radcliffe. "I'm not terribly interested in novels," Annie said, "but I did greatly admire *Pride and Prejudice*."

"I've read it three times. I confess I fell in love with Mr. Darcy and giggled excessively over Mr. Collins."

"I never thought of myself as a romantic until I read it."

"Who wouldn't fall in love with Mr. Darcy?" Dot had never given much thought to marrying until she read that book. And now she was ripe for matrimony and her own Mr. Darcy.

Her insides felt queasy when she recalled the awkwardness in the carriage the previous night when her husband-to-be did not want to kiss her.

"What do you prefer to read?" Annie asked.

"Papa says I have well-rounded reading taste, but then he imbues me with many qualities I don't possess." She shrugged her shoulders. "I will own a partiality to reading about history though I don't have a great fondness for the Greeks." She moved to a shelf that featured history tomes. "I thought I might enjoy Gibbons' *Rise and Decline of the Roman Empire*."

"All those volumes?"

Dot smiled. "Just the first today. It's in our library at Blandings, but I haven't read it. Now I fancy doing so." She picked up Volume One.

"I'm partial to Mr. Scott's historical novels myself."

"Oh, I do share your interest in those. When I finish Gibbons . . ." Dot laughed.

Annie selected Scott's newest novel, and the two moved to the attendant in order to process their books.

By the time they finished, Forrester stood on the pavement in front of the library, the family coach waiting. Dot thought he looked exceptionally fine today in a brown woolen coat the same colour as his hair. He wore it with buff breeches and soft leather boots that had obviously been polished that morning. A freshly starched cravat in white linen accentuated his straight white teeth. Even though his dress could not have been more casual, next to the other men moving through the streets of Bath, his tasteful elegance made him look like a king among beggars.

He addressed his sister. "I've come to collect my betrothed. I'll return you to Camden Crescent." He chuckled. "I brought the coach because I thought you'd be laden down with books and didn't want you to have to walk uphill with so heavy a load. Why the unusually light load?"

"Because Dot and I spoke endlessly of our similar taste in books. My soon-to-be-sister and I have a great deal in common when it comes to reading."

His smile brought an immediate softening of his features. "It has not escaped my observations that you two have a great deal in common, notwithstanding books."

The ladies exchanged amused glances. "How perceptive your brother is."

He handed first his sister into the coach, then Dot, whom he came to sit beside. He examined each lady's choice.

"Do you approve, sir?" Dot asked.

"I've not yet read Annie's book, so I cannot say." He eyed Dot's. "Why just the one volume of Gibbons?"

"Because I expect it will take quite some time to finish it. My father has the set in his library at Blandings."

"As do I at Hawthorne Manor."

"And you recommend it?"

"I found it fascinating reading. I'm just surprised that a . . . a woman would be interested in reading it."

Dot bristled. "You offend me."

"Yes, Timothy! Why should women not be permitted to read the same things men read?"

"They are permitted. It's just that I thought—yourself excluded, Annie—most women were interested in nothing but flowery poetry and gothic novels."

Annie glared at her brother. "Do not disparage flowery poetry!"

"There's nothing wrong with flowery poetry," Dot said.

Forrester held up his hands. "Forgive me. I can see I'm dealing with two exceptional young women who are possessed of most discerning taste in literature."

The ladies looked at one another and burst out laughing.

Then the coach slowed in front of the house on Camden Crescent, and Annie left them.

Forrester then took Dot's hand in his and pressed his lips to it. A quiver strummed through her. "I've instructed the coachman to take us to Ellie's lodgings."

His calling the dead girl by her Christian name made Dot even more aware that Ellie Macintosh had been a real person, a young woman who'd been full of life, a young woman Forrester had known, a young woman whose tragic death had saddened him.

* * *

While Ellie's street, Lower Richard, was not inhabited by the upper classes or even the upper middle classes, Appleton thought it most respectable looking, with its stone façades not altogether different from that of the city's more affluent addresses. Seeing a crested coach stop in front of Number 17 drew attention from the neighbors who were obviously unaccustomed to seeing such an occurrence in their neighborhood.

As he and Dot moved to the front door of Ellie's lodgings, he was pleased that she had dressed modestly in her simple sprigged muslin. Nothing about her shouted of affluence.

An aproned, stooped-over woman answered his knock on the door, which needed a fresh coat of paint. He handed her his card. "Lord Appleton to speak to the proprietress."

The old woman's eyes widened. She stood there for a moment, pondering if she should leave him standing on the step or invite him in. Obviously, she was unaccustomed to being called upon by a viscount. "Please, my lord, do come in while I give yer card to me mistress."

He signaled for Dot to enter first. The two of them awaited in the dark entry hall dominated by a narrow wooden staircase while the woman he assumed was the housekeeper entered a drawing room on the ground floor, shutting the door behind her.

She soon emerged from the chamber with a smile on her wrinkled face. "Mrs. Thorpe will see you now. Follow me, yer lordship, if you please." She went back into the drawing room.

The cream-coloured chamber was lighted from a single tall casement which faced the street and had been covered in draperies made of heavy linen the shade of celery. They crossed the room's bare wooden floors to face a middle-aged woman wearing a mob cap and sitting at a walnut writing table. She looked up to greet him. "Lord Appleton. Pray, do sit."

There was no sofa in the sparsely furnished room, only an olive green settee and several side chairs clinging to the walls. He would never be so rude as to greet a woman from a seated position. "You are Mrs. Thorpe?" he asked.

"Indeed, my lord." Her gaze flicked to Dot.

He nodded. "I should like to present you to Miss Dorothea Pankhurst."

The older woman offered a weak smile and nodded as her guests lowered themselves into the settee facing her.

Mrs. Thorpe did not waste time on pleasantries. "To what do I owe the honor of your visit, my lord?"

"Miss Pankhurst and I are most distressed over the recent . . . murder of your lodger, Miss Macintosh." A small prevarication, he decided, was needed. "She was our friend." Even though Dot had not been acquainted with the gaming hostess, she was as upset over her death as a friend would have been.

Mrs. Thorpe sighed heavily. "Dreadful business. I don't mind telling you I haven't been able to sleep since it 'appened. There's a murderer on the prowl, and he may come back. I keep my doors and windows locked day and night."

"As you should," he said. "You said *he may come back*. Does that mean that a man came here for Miss Macintosh the night she died?"

She shrugged her shoulders. "I can't say as Miss Macintosh ever had a man call 'ere for her. She was a good girl, she was. I don't run *that* kind of establishment. My ladies are not permitted to bring men onto these premises."

"We could tell you run a respectable establishment," Dot reassured.

"Do you know if Miss Macintosh had a special man that she saw?" he asked.

Mrs. Thorpe shook her head. "I 'ad no knowledge of it. During the three years she lived 'ere, there never seemed to be any man in her life. She worked nights, you see. And you could 'ave set your clock by the time she got home each night. She never dallied with her patrons after hours."

This visit wasn't yielding a single piece of information.

"Her last night on earth," Dot asked, "did she come home from work at the usual time?"

The landlady shook her head somberly, tears springing to her eyes. "She never came home that night. I learned from the newspaper she never even made it to work that night. I wonder if he waited for her 'ere."

Dot spoke morosely. "It's such a melancholy thing."

"Indeed it is," Mrs. Thorpe concurred.

"Tell me," Dot continued, "did Miss Macintosh have female friends who called?"

"Oh, yes. You can't expect a young person to spend all their time working and 'anging out in a bedchamber. One of the girls what worked with her would sometimes meet her 'ere, and they would go off for an outing. You see, the poor girl was an orphan. She didn't 'ave no one else in the world."

"Was it always the same girl who came here?" Dot asked.

Mrs. Thorpe thought for a moment. "Yes, I believe it was. A pretty little thing. Looked a lot like Miss Macintosh. About the same age and size, the only difference being her hair was ginger."

Appleton knew which girl it was. There was only one redhead in the employ of Mrs. Starr: Maryann.

Dot stood. "Are Miss Macintosh's possessions still here?"

Mrs. Thorpe clasped at her chest. "I 'aven't 'ad

the heart to go into that chamber."

"We should like to see them." Dot's voice softened. "Perhaps it would be easier on you if we accompany you, my dear Mrs. Thorpe."

The woman rose. "Indeed it would." Her voice cracked.

She proceeded to lead them up two flights of stairs to a small bedchamber in the garret. She then withdrew a key from her pocket and opened the door to the low-ceilinged room.

For so small a room it was well lighted from a dormer window that faced the street. A small oaken table fit perfectly into the dormer, a modest wooden chair tucked under it. The only other furnishings were a slender bed covered in a well-worn counterpane, a nightstand holding an oil lamp, and a skinny linen press of primitively painted wood.

The room was so tidy it looked almost as if Ellie's things had already been removed. Not a single wrinkle marred the bed covering, nor was even a piece of foolscap on the writing table. Only a pair of faded but pretty dresses hanging on wall hooks indicated that a young woman had occupied this chamber. Surprisingly, to him, not a single book could be seen. How did one live without the written word?

His hopes of finding letters that would reveal more about the dead woman and her circle of friends were dashed.

Dot opened the linen press that at one time must have been lime green, now faded to a greenish gray. It revealed that Ellie wasn't as neat as her room indicated. She must have been one of those persons who did not fancy observing clutter. Locked away in her linen press was what appeared to be her nightrail, her unmentionables, extra stockings and gloves, a summer hat, a Bible, and a small stack of correspondence.

It was difficult for him to suppress a smile.

Dot picked up the correspondence. Beneath it was a pouch that appeared to be coins. When Dot lifted it, it jingled. She dumped out its contents. It was a considerable sum.

Mrs. Thorp's eyes widened.

"I wouldn't have expected Miss Macintosh to have this much in her possession," Dot said as she began to count.

Appleton's head swayed from side to side almost as if he were in a daze. "Neither would I." He could not remove his eyes from the generous heap of coins.

"I do declare! There are almost fifty guineas here," Dot exclaimed. "Here, Mrs. Thorpe. Whatever money Miss Macintosh had should go to you."

The older woman smiled broadly as she took the bulging pouch. "I 'ad no idea the poor girl managed to save this much money."

"Do you think, Mrs. Thorpe, seeing as how we were Miss Macintosh's friends and seeing that you're now paid up on any rents owed, do you think Lord Appleton and I could take these letters and our dear friend's Bible so we'd have something personal of hers, something to keep to remember her by? I doubt they'd be worth anything to anyone else."

Mrs. Thorpe gripped the pouch greedily, a smile on her face. "I should be happy for you two to have those things what belonged to Miss Macintosh."

Dot felt the pockets of the dead woman's

garments but found nothing. Appleton looked under the bed and under the mattress to the same result. There were no rugs on the floor or pictures on the wall under which something could have been hidden. There was nowhere else in the chamber where Ellie could have hidden anything.

He couldn't help but wonder how in the devil Ellie had been able to get her hands on so much money. For one of her station, fifty guineas was a fortune. Even for a woman like Mrs. Thorpe, who owned a well-situated house, it was a lot of money.

As they made their way downstairs, he casually asked, "Do you know, Mrs. Thorpe, one of the seamstresses at Miss Pankhurst's dressmaker's was inquiring about lodgings. Do you object to telling us what a situation like Miss Macintosh's would cost? We'd like to tell her about your house since she needs a respectable place to live."

"Seven pounds a month with meals furnished."

"And I'm certain the food here must be very good," Dot said.

* * *

As soon as they were in the carriage, he thought aloud. "How in the devil did Ellie get her hands on that much money?"

"I don't know if we'll ever know, but it must have something to do with her death."

He eyed Dot, thankful that if he had to spend the rest of his life with her, he wasn't going to be tied down to a woman in want of brains. "Then you don't think her murder was random?"

"It's possible there's a maniac running about Bath intent on killing young women, but now that we've seen the hoard of money she hid away I'm highly suspicious her murderer was someone she knew."

"I am, too." He'd instructed the coachman to take them to Camden Crescent where he and Dot could peruse Ellie's papers in private. He only hoped Annie didn't come barging in. For some peculiar reason, he did not want his sister to know what he and Dot were investigating—peculiar because he and Annie had always shared everything.

It wasn't that Dot was usurping his sister. It was more that he felt he was already jeopardizing one woman he cared about. He did not want to put Annie in danger too.

After all, a homicidal sex maniac might be on the prowl in their city.

Dot shook Ellie's Bible. A slip of paper fell from it. Their eyes met, and then she picked it up and read it, her brows forming a deep V.

"What's it say?"

"Nothing. It's your name."

"Let me see." On a small sheet of torn paper, written in a feminine hand, were the words *Lord Appleton*. He looked up at her. "I wish to God I knew what that means."

"Were you being honest with me?" She drilled him with those almost-black eyes.

He gave her a puzzled look. "About not seeing Ellie away from Mrs. Starr's?"

Dot nodded.

"I told you the truth. I can't think why she would have written my name."

"Perhaps she fancied you." Dot smiled. "You *are* most dashing."

He returned her smile. "Thank you, my love, but I assure you Miss Macintosh never favored me in any way. In fact, it was at her hands, whilst she was dealing, that I had the most lamentable night of my life."

"Oh, dear, I am sorry for that."

"That night cured me of a lifelong habit of gambling."

"Many men swear off gambling, only to weaken."

He stiffened. Their eyes locked. He could only barely control his anger. "I have never in my life gone back on my word."

"It's gratifying to know you're a man of your word." Her voice then softened. "I'm sorry if I sounded as if I don't trust you, but remember we haven't known each other very long."

He nodded solemnly.

When they reached Appleton House, they quietly made their way to his library, closed the door, and sat beside one another at the writing table to look over Ellie's papers.

The first piece of correspondence they read was a letter dated nearly four years earlier. Ellie would have been around sixteen. After reading a few paragraphs, Appleton realized it had been written by Ellie's cruel stepmother shortly after Ellie's father died.

The woman said now that Ellie was a woman she was expected to make her own way in the world, that this woman, whose name was Eliza, had no further use for her as she had her own children to feed. It was also hinted at that Ellie's beauty—though the woman was too mean-spirited to compliment her—would prevent her own daughters from finding husbands.

It sickened him to think of Ellie having been thrown out alone in the world at so tender an age.

"How heartbreaking," Dot said.

All he could do was nod solemnly as he met his fiancée's watery gaze. It comforted him that Dot was possessed of tender feelings.

The next letter was from a parish priest in Devon giving the date of Ellie Macintosh's baptism. Appleton's heart fell. The poor girl must have carried this around in the hopes of needing it when she got married.

The last paper they unfolded was a piece of parchment upon which was printed the Ten Commandments. In script at the top, someone had written: *Presented to Ellie Macintosh, for Highest Achievement in Recitation of Biblical Verse.*

Curiously, in another hand at the bottom, was written, *I am not worthy.*

"What do you make of that?" she asked.

"I don't know, but I believe she wrote that on the bottom recently. See, the ink has not faded in the least, not like the ink at the top."

"I believe you're right."

He swallowed. "And I believe that guilt has something to do with her murder."

She nodded solemnly. "We need to question Mrs. Thorpe's neighbors. It's possible someone saw Miss Macintosh with her killer."

"Good idea. How about tomorrow?"

"We would need to wait until late in the day, owing to the fact it's a working class neighborhood."

"Yes," he said with a nod. "If we hope to reach more the neighbors, coming later in the day *would* be more helpful."

"And don't forget, you must bring many of your calling cards. That will impress them."

"Clever lady, you are." Her father's praise had not been tinged by parental pride. It was the bloody truth. "I shall see you late in the day tomorrow."

Chapter 10

Laden with packages, Sir Elvin was just returning home from an outing with his sisters when Appleton arrived at his house. It was but a brisk walk between their two houses, and it felt good to stretch his legs. Appleton disliked coach rides, especially in the eminently walkable city of Bath.

Sir Elvin gave him a mock glare. "So you've actually found time to call on your oldest friend?"

Appleton felt beastly that he'd offered for Dot and even told others at the musical without first telling his closest friend. That was partly why he'd come here this afternoon after escorting Dot home. He slapped Sir Elvin on the back. "I always have time for you, old fellow."

"Can I interest you in a glass of Madera?"

"I'll pour it myself while you finish up with your sisters." Appleton went straight to Elvin's library. The room looked vastly different than it had when Elvin's twin still lived at home. Then, Melvin typically took over the chamber, and piles of books were stacked everywhere. Most of the books were now gone, Melvin having taken them to his bride's home on the Royal Crescent. The Royal Crescent library had since become the book-filled study where Melvin spent at least twelve hours a day on books he researched and authored.

Appleton poured out two glasses and went to sit on a high-backed chair near the smoldering fire. As the day had warmed, the need for a fire had decreased.

When Sir Elvin entered the chamber, Appleton held out his port. "These women can exhaust one."

"Indeed." Sir Elvin came to sit in a chair identical to the one upon which Appleton sat. He took a long swig. "I'm rather out of charity with women at present. First, one stole my brother away, and now I'm losing you."

Appleton shook his head. "It's not like that at all. You're one of those who told me I had to marry an heiress. I had no choice. I'm doing this for my family. You'd do the same."

Elvin did not respond for a moment. "But I wouldn't race off and offer for the heiress without telling you. After all, I'm closer to you than to anyone on earth—except my twin."

"Forgive me. I realize I should have informed you of my decision."

"Why such a bloody hurry?"

"Because I had reason to believe word was getting out about Miss Pankhurst's fortune, and I feared her drawing room would turn into a bloody mob of suitors."

Elvin gave him a quizzing stare. "And you don't have confidence that you could have won her affections amongst a broad field of admirers?"

"I had no desire to prolong the courtship. I'd made up my mind and was ready to act on my decision."

"Then you have no doubts? No regrets?"

Of course he had regrets! He'd longed to marry a beautiful woman who captivated him the same way Glee had bewitched Blanks or Catherine Bexley had won Melvin's undying devotion.

But he vowed to never mention those regrets to anyone. He owed Dot that much respect. "I have found that Miss Pankhurst and I suit very well, and I'm a most fortunate man."

He actually *was* most fortunate to have secured the lady's hand. Had he not met her on the precise day he did, someone else might have snared her affections. Thank God for that bloody cat of hers!

"My only regret is that you feel things will change between you and me." Appleton's gaze locked with Elvin's. "They won't. You'll always be my closest friend. And confidant."

Elvin drank up. "Then I've behaved like a bloody woman."

They both laughed. "God, don't say that. You're my respite from the fair sex—with whom I've spent far too much time as of late."

"I must say there's been a remarkable transformation in your intended. Misjudged her. She does credit to her gender. Wouldn't know she'd not always mingled with the likes of our sisters."

Sir Elvin regarded his friend, amusement flashing in his dark eyes. "I am given to understand she attended the musical last night *without* her cats."

Appleton really did not appreciate anyone, not even his closest friend, thinking Dot peculiar. "I believe the lady's excessive attachment to her felines was encouraged because of her isolation. She's an only child. Now she has me, Annie, and many new friends that should supplant those demmed cats."

"Good to know. Didn't like to think of you toting around those cats."

"There are some things at which I will draw the line."

Laughing, Elvin got up to refill their glasses. "How can you possibly have anything in common with a lass from Lincolnshire?"

"Surprisingly, we get along far better than I had expected. In fact, she intrinsically understood how upset I was about Ellie's death. Even though she'd never met her, she has been very disturbed over the murder."

"What woman wouldn't be?" Sir Elvin shook his head. "I can't dispel it from my thoughts. Such a terrible thing. It's the kind of tragedy one might expect in London, but not here in Bath, and not to someone we saw regularly. Ellie was so pretty. And young. Terrible pity."

"Did you ever hear of her mixing with any of the patrons outside of Mrs. Starr's?"

Elvin's eyes rounded. "Ellie? Never. There was something . . . well, something innocent about her."

Appleton nodded. "I too felt that way about her." He hesitated a moment, then decided to share with Elvin the inquiries he and Dot had made. "I found out from Mrs. Starr where she lived, and Dot and I went there."

"I take it Dot is Miss Pankhurst?"

"Yes."

"Whatever did you go to Ellie's for?"

"Miss Pankhurst feels it's our duty to bring the murderer to justice."

Elvin's brows scrunched together. "She knows who he is?"

"Good lord, no! But it's our aim to discover his

identity."

"Sounds bloody dangerous. The blighter's killed once already!"

"Be assured I won't let Dot out of my sight."

"*You* are not invincible! Looks like I'm not going to be able to let *you* out of *my* sight!" Elvin took a long sip of Madera. "So what did you learn at Ellie's lodgings?"

Appleton told him everything they'd discovered.

"There's no way Ellie could have saved up fifty pounds on the pittance Mrs. Starr gives her girls," Elvin said, "and we know Ellie wasn't interested in earning money in other ways."

"I will own, it's highly suspicious, but the only explanation is that she likely *did* earn money and likely from one of the patrons of Mrs. Starr's. Now we have to find out who he was."

"Maryann must know. Apparently Maryann was her closest—and possibly her only—friend. Do you want me to speak to her?" Elvin asked.

"No. Dot and I will. I wish you could have seen the clever way Dot handled the landlady. I will need you to speak to Maryann for us and set up a meeting since I refuse to step foot in a gaming establishment ever again."

Elvin looked at him as if he'd suddenly sprouted a halo. "You really were serious?"

"Have you ever in these past twenty plus years that you've known me known me to go back on my word?"

Elvin pondered the question a moment, and then shook his head. "You're the most truthful fellow I know, save for Melvin."

Appleton stood. "So you'll speak to Maryann about meeting us?"

"I will." Elvin got up. "There's something else I

wanted to ask you."

"Yes?"

"What do you plan to do about Mrs. Pratt?"

Appleton sighed and sank back into the chair. "I'd forgotten all about her."

"How does one forget about one's mistress?"

"Since the night I lost my fortune, I've had more important things on my mind. There was also the fact that I had no money with which to either maintain her or to give her a parting settlement. Still don't."

Nodding, Sir Elvin grabbed the decanter and poured out two more glasses. "Those problems will be solved once you're married and acquire the Pankhurst wealth."

Appleton slowly shook his head. "I can't use Dot's money to keep a mistress, you idiot!"

Elvin's lips puckered. "You can't?"

"Course not. And even if I had my own money, being an unfaithful bridegroom would make me feel like a traitor."

"Like you thought your father a traitor to your mother?"

"Good lord, did I tell you that?"

Elvin nodded. "When you were quite young—and far more religious than you are now."

Appleton might sometimes think like a bloody moralist, but he no longer went around lambasting those who didn't. After all, he had his reputation as a profligate to uphold.

He just hoped Dot hadn't learned of that.

He sighed. "I believe I *will* have that glass of Madera."

He did need to consider what to do about Mrs. Pratt.

* * *

"What, pray tell, is that sedan chair doing in our entry hall?" Dot demanded, eyeing her father impatiently.

In his usual armchair near the fire, his feet resting on an upholstered stool, Mr. Pankhurst looked up at her, a sheepish expression on his face. "'Tis a shame to waste two such strapping footmen when the act of getting around this hilly city is so difficult for one with my infirmities. Gives them something to do, carrying me to and from the baths and such."

She put her hands to hips and glared at him. "We came to Bath to get you well, not to make you even more of an invalid. You will become so reliant on the chair, you'll become a cripple. Is that what you want? At nine-and-forty? To be a frail, reclusive old man?" She knew she was being harsh, but it was the only way to treat him.

He was like a spoiled child accustomed to always getting his own way, and like a child, he did not always make decisions that were in his best interest. Lamentably, because he'd been born to great wealth, he'd always been uncommonly lazy. Even too lazy to walk.

Her father effected a persecuted expression. "Of course I don't choose to be an invalid. You have no idea how I long for the days of my youth when I was fit. I don't mind telling you I was one mean cricket player! And I wasn't half bad at boxing and fencing and any manner of young men's pursuits that required physical stamina." He sighed. "And now walking has become an ordeal."

She came to sit on a chair facing him and spoke in a more tender voice. "I don't mean to be an ogre, but it's my belief you've brought much of this infirmity upon yourself."

"How can you say that? How cruel!"

"I believe one of the reasons walking's an ordeal is because you do so little of it, your bones and muscles cry out from disuse. The best thing for you is activity."

She prayed she was right, that she was not misjudging a potentially chronic condition of her father's. "And I truly believe that your penchant for brandy exacerbates problems, like gout, that contribute to painful walking."

His eyes narrowed. "Fiddlefudge!"

She shrugged. "You're not only hurting yourself. You're hurting me. I love you. And what about my future children? Would you deprive them of . . ." The very notion of losing her father caused tears to spring to her eyes.

Topham entered the chamber and stood just inside the doorway, erect as the king's own sentries. "A Mrs. Blankenship is calling, sir. She has brought two small persons with her and says she has come to see the kittens."

Dot popped up from her seat, swiped at her moist eyes, and turned to her father. "How delightful! You be all that is gracious to the lady whilst I gather up my kitties." Only Nellie was currently in the drawing room, curled up sleeping on the window seat.

Which Mrs. Blankenship was calling, Dot fleetingly wondered, but decided it must be Glee since she had broached the subject of bringing her son and daughter to visit Dot's cats.

Locating three more cats might not be an easy task. She quickly found Preenie Queenie curled up on a window seat, this one in Dot's bedchamber, the sun almost sparkling off her white fur.

But Dot was having no luck finding Lover Boy or Fur Blossom.

Then she saw that the chambermaid must have left her father's bedchamber door open. That would be an invitation to her curious cats, who were not permitted in her father's rooms. She followed her instincts and quickly saw Fur Blossom's glossy black-and-white fur coiled into Papa's wash basin. "Come, you naughty kitty," she said as she picked up the cat.

Someone had left open the drawer to her father's desk, and that silly Lover Boy had tried to stuff his fat orange body into the drawer half his size. She had to laugh.

Moments later, she strolled into the drawing room carrying Lover Boy and Fur Blossom. She was surprised that it was the elder Mrs. Blankenship who had brought her grandchildren.

When the children looked up and saw her with the two cats, they squealed with delight.

"Why do you not sit down so we can put a cat in each of your laps?" Dot suggested.

The lovely little girl, who looked about five and who vastly resembled her fiery-haired mother, almost flew to the sofa, then patted the spot next to her for her little brother to come sit.

And little he was! The lad obviously could not yet talk and had only just learned to walk. With dark hair and eyes, he was the image of his father. Dot could well understand how the parents and grandmother could dote on such adorable children.

"This cat's name is Lover Boy," Dot said as she placed him on the little girl's lap.

The little girl giggled.

When the little boy went to pet Lover Boy, his

sister snapped at him. "This one's mine."

"And this is yours." Dot placed Fur Blossom on the lad's lap. His little hands immediately began to stroke the cat's soft hair. "Her name is Fur Blossom," Dot said in a softened voice.

"That's a silly name," the little girl said. Then she eyed her brother and slowly pronounced the word "Kitty" in an attempt to extend his vocabulary while she went to pet the animal.

"Mine!" he said.

Dot could see he'd learned at least one word.

"Children, allow me to introduce you to Mr. Pankhurst's daughter, Miss Pankhurst," their grandmother said. Turning to Dot, she placed a hand on the little girl's shoulder. "This is my granddaughter Joy." Then she settled a gentle hand on the little boy's dark hair. "This is my grandson we still call Little Gregory."

"He certainly resembles his father. How old is he?"

"Fifteen months."

"I daresay that's still a baby," Mr. Pankhurst said.

Dot directed her attention at the little girl. "And how old are you, Joy?"

"Four and a half."

Before Dot left to find Nellie, she observed that her father had removed his feet from the stool and sat erect. He looked far more vibrant.

"I've one more cat to fetch," Dot said. "I cannot vouch for how long these cats will behave themselves. Perhaps with four from which to choose we can manage two on decent behavior."

When she returned with Nellie, her father and Mrs. Blankenship scarcely noticed. They were deep in conversation.

It occurred to Dot they were not very far apart in age. Blanks was the same age as Forrester—thirty. But now that she thought about it, hadn't someone said something about this woman being Blanks' stepmother? Yet she was old enough to have a son who was married to a woman in their circle. So she had to be close to Dot's father's age.

This lady did look exceedingly handsome for a woman in her mid-forties. She had far fewer gray hairs in her dark brown hair than Dot's father, and she had not gone to fat. And, like all those Dot had mingled with since she'd been in Bath, this woman dressed in excellent taste.

While Dot played with the children and the cats, she pondered her father. Had the isolation back at Blandings contributed to his malaise? Judging from the lively way he was conversing with this woman, he must have missed being around people of his own age and background.

Coming to Bath had been the best thing they had ever done. For her father—and especially for Dot.

Now she needed to integrate him into the city's social activities.

Mrs. Blankenship tossed a glance at the assemblage of cats. "My but you have several—and they're all vastly different."

Dot nodded. As much as she loved others to admire her cats, she needed to be a better hostess.

Fur Blossom suddenly leapt from Baby Gregory's lap, and the tot attempted to run after her.

Dot disturbed the sleeping Nellie. "Here, Gregory. Why don't you make friends with this kitty? Come sit on the floor." She patted the floor.

He came and plopped down on the Turkey carpet in front of the hearth, and Dot placed Nellie on his lap. She kept her hand there a moment, stroking the cat in the hopes of keeping Nellie from abandoning the little boy.

"What's that cat's name?" Joy asked.

"This is Nellie."

Joy picked up Lover Boy and hugged him. "So they're all girls except my Lover Boy?"

"That's right."

"Do you get to sleep with your kitties?" Joy asked.

Dot nodded.

"I wish I had a kitty," little Joy said in a forlorn voice. "In the country, we are permitted to have dogs, but they live outdoors."

"Have you ever asked for a kitty?"

Joy shrugged. "I'm going to go home and ask for one today. I think I'll ask Papa. He never tells me *no*."

Dot laughed to herself. That tall, handsome Gregory "Blanks" Blankenship was easily commanded by his tiny, adored four-year-old daughter.

She felt a fluttering in her breast. Would Forrester ever be similarly smitten over a daughter Dot might one day bear him? The very notion turned her insides to porridge.

The children played with the cats for another ten minutes before their grandmother stood. First she turned to Dot. "I neglected to offer felicitations on your forthcoming nuptials to Lord Appleton. What a wonderful match it is for both of you. I was very happy to learn of it from Glee after she attended the musical."

"Thank you," Dot said. "I'm rather happy

myself."

"We need to go now, children, but perhaps Mr. and Miss Pankhurst will permit us to come again?" Mrs. Blankenship eyed Dot's father.

"It will be our pleasure," he said. He then stood and walked them to the door without the slightest sign of a limp.

Once they were gone, Dot took up the afternoon's edition of the *Bath Chronicle* and returned to the drawing room to sit before the window and read it where the light was best. Lover Boy came to curl up in her lap.

Her father, too, came to sit near her, his customary glass of brandy in his hand. "I found the Blankenship children to be well behaved."

She nodded. "I wish my kitties behaved as nicely."

"Mrs. Blankenship is a most handsome woman. Wouldn't you agree?"

Dot set down her newspaper and regarded her father. This was the first time in her life he had ever taken notice of a woman's appearance. "I certainly would. In fact, I'm surprised some widower has not snatched her up. It's my understanding she's been widowed for a few years."

"Yes, she told me her late husband has been gone for six years."

"It seemed to me the two of you did not want for conversation."

"Indeed. She's remarkably easy to talk to. It's as if I've known her for quite some time, like we're old friends."

"I daresay it's because you have a great deal in common."

"I believe you're right, but then you always are."

"The next time we go to an assembly or a musical at night, we must see that Mrs. Blankenship also comes," Dot suggested.

"A capital idea!"

How happy it made her to see her father in such good humor. She picked up her paper and continued reading. First, she looked for news about Ellie Macintosh's murder. There was no new information, only sensational interviews with women thoroughly convinced they were to be the next victims of the evil madman.

When she finished that, she turned to another page. Even though she knew very few people in Bath, she enjoyed reading the silly Society column that was always filled with scandalous tidbits. Today's mentioned a *certain flirtation observed at the Pump Room between a Mrs. A____y and a Mr. P-----n*. Then she read one that caused her heartbeat to roar.

What will Mrs. Pr__t think if it's true her Lord A__le__n is truly to wed the city's newest heiress?

Now all those things Dot had previously read about Forrester being a profligate came rushing back. Was it not said he kept a mistress? A Mrs. Surname Beginning with the Letter P? Would he keep his mistress after they were married? Dot's breath stilled. Was he lying with his mistress right now?

Dot could not marry a man who was an unfaithful husband.

Chapter 11

Appleton crumpled the paper. It simply would not do to dismiss Betsy Pratt with a letter. After all, she had been his mistress for the past two years. He thought. He wasn't very good with dates, and it wasn't as if he spent very much time with her.

It wasn't as if one went about in public with a woman of that sort. He had three young sisters to consider. And it wasn't as if Mrs. Pratt was the kind of woman one wished to spend a great deal of time with. She was pretty enough. And obliging enough. But the woman, who was some half a dozen years older than he, was as dull as a wooden spoon.

There was nothing to do but to go to her tonight and explain the reversal in his fortunes which necessitated a break between them. First he penned a letter to the woman he'd rather go to tonight, the woman whose fortune would rescue his family from ruin. He needed to notify Dot that he would not be seeing her until the next day when they'd go back to Ellie's street.

With Digby's assistance, he made himself agreeable looking and presented himself at Mrs. Pratt's modest but most respectable looking house east of the river not long after dark. "Good evening, my lord," her butler said, swinging open the door from him to enter. It was clear from the tone of the butler's voice he was surprised to see Appleton. It had been quite a while since he'd last visited Betsy Pratt.

"I shall tell Mrs. Pratt you're here. Permit me to show you to the drawing room."

Though small, the lady's drawing room was tastefully furnished with a Turkey carpet on the floor and scarlet draperies at the single narrow window. The draperies were not of costly silk but of a cheaper fabric that mimicked it. A single sofa in the same scarlet fabric faced the fire where a mantelpiece featured a fine wooden case clock on balled feet.

Instead of sitting, he paced the chamber.

A few minutes later, she entered. "My lord! I've missed you most dreadfully. Have you not come rather early tonight? I am delighted, of course. Shall we go upstairs?"

He looked at her. Even though she was not in mourning, she wore black. That was to perpetuate the myth she was a widow when in fact she had never been married.

Her hair had been a shade of medium brown. Why had he never noticed how many gray strands had woven into it? There was an artificial look about her. Some kind of white powder covered her face and made her look even older, and she'd darkened her cheeks with bright red rouge.

He supposed he'd not noticed these things before because he and she normally spent their time together in her bedchamber with only the light from a single taper or the fire.

Then, too, he'd been more interested in her figure, which he found pleasing, owing to his appreciation of a generous bosom—the only physical trait this woman shared with his betrothed.

Just being here with Mrs. Pratt made him feel unclean, unworthy of Dot. Just being here with Betsy Pratt made him appreciate the purity of the woman he planned to marry. In addition to Dot's innocence, she was possessed of a tender heart unrestricted by a person's rank.

He did not presume to harshly judge Mrs. Pratt because of the misfortune of her birth. He was certain she had many good qualities, too. But comparing her to Dot was like contrasting coal to diamonds.

He was not worthy of Miss Dorothea Pankhurst.

"I can't go upstairs with you," he said, his voice firm. "I've come to tell you I can't see you anymore. I've lost every farthing. It's fortuitous that I was able to pay the lease on your house through the end of the year—before I lost my fortune."

Her eyes moistened, which made him feel beastly.

"I will endeavor to endorse you to my gentlemen friends," he added.

She nodded. "I'll miss you."

He drew a deep breath and put even more distance between them. Then he turned and walked away. He would have felt less guilty were he in a position to offer her a financial settlement, but at present he wasn't even in a position to dower his sisters.

* * *

The clouds and cool winds outside did little to lift Dot's spirits the following day when Mr. Gibby came for a final dancing lesson before the next assembly. She had looked forward to dancing skillfully in one of her beautiful new dresses with the handsome peer to whom she was betrothed.

But gloom filled her heart as well as the chamber in which they practiced their dance steps. She'd had a wretched night. Sleep eluded her as she tortured herself imagining Forrester in the arms of his mistress.

She wondered if Mrs. Surname Beginning with P was beautiful. How long had the woman been under Forrester's protection? Was he in love with her? Had he offered for Dot merely to secure her fortune?

This was the first time since Dot had come to Bath that she regretted having left her home in Lincolnshire. For if she had stayed at Blandings, she would not be suffering like this. She and her kitties would have slept soundly in her bed without a care in the world.

"I sincerely hope, Miss Pankhurst, that you will be merrier at the next assembly," Mr. Gibby said as she moped along an imaginary longway with him.

"Don't know what's gotten into my gal," Mr. Pankhurst said. "Any other young lady who'd just become betrothed to the best matrimonial prize in all of Bath and who was wearing such fashionable attire—not to mention having been instructed in dance by the city's finest dancing master—would be looking forward with delight to Tuesday's assembly. You do know, do you not, Mr. Gibby, that my daughter is betrothed to Lord Appleton?"

"Indeed I had heard, and I cannot convey what an honor it is to have the future Lady Appleton as my patron." He shrugged. "Perhaps Miss Pankhurst's reticence is merely because she's shy.

This will be your first assembly, yes?"

She shook her head. "Second, actually, though I was not really at liberty to dance at the first."

"Now you will be as accomplished a dancer as any young lady in the highest social circles in all of Bath," Mr. Gibby said. "Even in London, I daresay."

She should be comforted by his praise, but it wasn't as if she were worried about her reception at Tuesday night's assembly. Whether strangers thought well of her mattered little. What mattered to her was Forrester's feelings—especially toward his purported mistress.

At some point before they married she would have to bring up the subject of his mistress because she could never countenance an unfaithful husband. Even if it meant she would have to break the engagement.

The time for such a conversation, though, was not now. She wasn't sure if Forrester had even become comfortable with the notion of being married. It was harder for men, especially men who were thirty years of age, to easily adjust to such a complete change in their lives. It would take time.

For the last few minutes of her lesson, she forced a smile simply to please her patient dance master and her indulgent father.

After Mr. Gibby left she reminded her father that he must accompany her Tuesday night. "I should love to see you dance with Mrs. Blankenship."

He perked up. "Will she be attending?"

"I'm not precisely sure, but think how disappointed you'd be if you didn't go and you found out the next day that she went and you weren't there. I believe she'd be very disappointed, too."

"Do you really think so?" he asked.

"Indeed I do."

* * *

"Should we again take your coach to Lower Richard Street?" Dot asked Appleton late that following afternoon.

He was unable to suppress a smile as he stood there observing her. She held one of those cats of hers in the most adoring manner. He couldn't say which one it was. The only one he knew was that annoying orange male cat whose name he refused to repeat.

It was as if thinking about the wretched creature signaled him to come and rub himself against Appleton's leg.

He ignored it.

Over these past two weeks Appleton had come to understand a good bit about the workings of Dot's mind. "Knowing you, my dear one, you've analyzed this and have a mental list of reasons for and against taking my coach."

She giggled. "That is true. If we arrive in your aristocratic coach, it will draw attention from those on the modest street who are not accustomed to seeing a carriage of the nobility calling upon their neighbors. Because of that, I believe it may be easier for us to find residents who will be willing to talk to some fancy lord."

He tossed his head back and laughed.

"On the other hand," she continued, her eyes narrowing at his joviality, "if we act like we don't consider ourselves above them—though really it's only you who is actually above them in station—they might speak more candidly. Those not accustomed to the nobility could be too shy to speak to said fancy lord."

"As said fancy lord, I'd like to weigh in on this. I tend to agree with your idea of arriving in the coach. I have found it does tend to draw attention from those in the lower classes—none of whom have I ever felt were too shy to speak with me."

"But you didn't come in your coach."

"There is that," he said with a shrug. He leaned into her and pressed a kiss upon her cheek.

Why had he gone and done that? He'd not ever kissed her before. Now that it was done, he felt awkward, but at the time it seemed perfectly natural. Recovering quickly, he added, "My betrothed appears to be far more analytical than I."

The unexpectedness of the kiss must have stolen her tongue, which was uncharacteristic for Dot. She looked downward. "Oh, look how much Lover Boy loves you, Forrester! How can you not want to pick him up and get a good kitty cuddle?"

A kitty cuddle? Spare him, please. He peered downward. "My valet would have apoplexy if I allow cat hair on my dark coat."

She put down her black and white cat. "You sound just like my Papa."

He assisted with her fur-trimmed cloak, and they left to walk back to Appleton House on Camden Crescent to fetch his coach. Neither spoke at first. Was she, too, pondering his spontaneous cheek kiss? It only now occurred to him that this was the fourth day since she had agreed to marry him, and he'd never kissed her.

Having never been betrothed before, he had no knowledge of how one did act with the woman one meant to wed. Of course, were he in love with her, he would have taken her in his arms and properly kissed her on the mouth when she consented to become his wife.

When it occurred to him that his failure to kiss her might have offended Dot, he almost stopped dead in his footsteps. He'd rather sever a limb than hurt her. He might not be in love with Dot, but he most certainly had come to care about her. She was eminently admirable.

Because she had consented to marry him, it must mean that she fancied him. Therefore, it would stand to reason she would wish to be kissed by the man she favored.

What a complete oaf I've been! Kissing shouldn't be something one had to contemplate. Just like back at her house, he'd kissed her because he bloody well wanted to, because he enjoyed being with her, and being with her made him happy. That's why he'd so spontaneously leaned over and pecked her on the cheek.

He vowed that henceforth he would make a conscious effort to kiss her when leaving her each night.

A pity he didn't lust after her. It would have made the prospect of their marriage much more appealing.

He looked down at her delicate hand resting on his proffered sleeve, and he covered it with his. The idea of being married no longer revolted him. He could have done far worse than marrying Miss Dorothea Pankhurst.

She looked up at him with those soulful dark eyes and smiled.

Then he lifted her hand and pressed his lips to it. "I am happy that the woman with whom I'm going to share life sees eye to eye with me much of the time."

"And I'm happy that the man with whom I'm going to share my life does not treat me as if I'm empty headed." Her amused gaze met his. "Most of the time."

"When have I not?"

Her eyebrows lifted. "That day when you picked Annie and me up from the lending library."

An aggravated expression on his face, he nodded. "Forgive me for initially thinking your taste in books would parallel that of most maidens—many of whom *are* empty headed. I should have known if Annie got on so well with you, you couldn't be stupid."

"Surely you haven't forgotten all my father's accolades," she said with a laugh. "Does he not sufficiently praise me?"

"I have found his praise to be well founded."

"I believe you're prevaricating again, my lord. And now that you've been properly chastised, I must make a confession."

He turned to her. The chilled air had turned her cheeks red, something he hadn't expected to see in one with her dark colouring. He thought again of that Italian opera singer whose colouring was very similar to Dot's and to whom he'd been so attracted. "You thought I would be stupid?"

She shrugged. "I hadn't actually considered whether you'd be intelligent."

"But you were expecting me to be . . . surely you didn't think I was as bad at that blasted *Bath Chronicle* paints me?"

She nodded sheepishly. "I thought you would be quite dissipated. A profligate, to be sure."

His stomach dropped. She'd no doubt read that he kept a mistress. He hoped to God she did not bring that up. He cleared his throat. "So, it's certainly a cold day today."

She laughed at his efforts to redirect the conversation. "Indeed. I believe we'll welcome a ride in your carriage."

Once they were in his coach, they arrived at Lower Richard Street in just a few minutes. She turned to him. "You did bring your calling cards?"

"I'm a most obedient husband-to-be."

"I shall take comfort in that."

"Where do you think we should begin? I'm sure you'll have thought it out."

"Indeed. We ought to start at Mrs. Thorpe's next-door neighbors on either side." As she spoke, she peered from his coach window. "I see that the arrival of your coach has already resulted in more than one curtain being lifted."

"Good."

A moment later, he was knocking upon the front door of the house west of Mrs. Thorpe's. Customarily, one of his rank employed his coachman to knock and announce him, but he thought these working class people might not be acquainted with the ways of the nobility. Better to come himself. That might even establish a more casual atmosphere in which to question the neighbor.

A middle-aged woman whose brown hair was streaked with gray opened the door warily.

Appleton presented her with his calling card. "Good day to you. Allow me to introduce myself. I'm Lord Appleton, and I wished to make inquiries about a young lady who resided next door to you."

It seemed apparent to him the woman did not know whether she should invite him in, or if she should keep him on the step. She chose the latter.

"The pretty one what was murdered?"

"Yes." He bowed his head reverently. "My fiancée," he indicated Dot, "and I were acquainted with the lady and distressed over her death. We wondered if you ever saw her with a man."

The woman shook her head. "Never. And I wondered about her not having a fellow, seeing as she was such a pretty girl."

"Did you ever see any man loiter around this street?"

"Loiter?"

This neighbor must not know the meaning of the word. "Did you ever see a man hanging about?" he asked.

She pursed her lips. "I don't think so. I believe I'd have noticed if there was some deranged sex maniac 'anging about."

He wasn't surprised. "Do others reside here, others whom we could question?"

"Just me husband now, and he has trouble walking. He's a shut-in and can't even make it to the window to peer out."

"Well, we thank you for your time," he said.

"If you should think of anything," Dot said, "please contact his lordship."

The woman looked again at his card. "I've read about Lord Appleton in the *Bath Chronicle*! Fancy getting to meet you myself!"

"I beg that you not judge me by what is written in that newspaper," he said with a smile and a wink.

"He's really a very nice man," Dot said. They bid farewell and walked to the house on the other side of Mrs. Thorpe's.

At that house they got the opportunity to question three different persons, but none of them had ever seen Ellie with a man, and none had ever seen any suspicious men in the neighborhood.

"I suggest we try across the street," Dot said. "Those people can more easily peer from their windows to watch the comings and goings from Mrs. Thorpe's establishment."

They met with no more success at the first two houses they tried, but got a glimmer of encouragement at the third where an elderly woman invited them in and asked them to sit in her parlor. She introduced herself as Mrs. Flint and said she'd lived alone since her husband had died twelve years earlier. Her cluttered parlor was similar in layout to Mrs. Thorpe's sparsely furnished chamber.

"Now what can I help you with?" the old lady asked.

Appleton went into his practiced query.

Her brows lowered. "I was aware of the young girl who lodged with Mrs. Thorpe. She was—as you know—uncommonly pretty. I'd been noticing her for . . . I'd say about three years. And not once in those three years did I ever see a young fellow call on her. Of course, Mrs. Thorpe is noted for keeping a respectable establishment. But now that you bring it up, I did see the pretty lodger with a man at Sydney Gardens about two weeks ago."

It was difficult to contain his excitement. "Can you describe him?"

She shook her head. "Not really. You see, I was some distance away. I knew it was her, though, because I'd seen her leave her house not long before I left mine. She was wearin' a blue dress."

Appleton suddenly recalled that Ellie had been wearing a blue dress the night he lost his fortune.

"Had he called on her at the house?" he asked.

"No. She left alone. I had the impression she was meeting him at Sydney Gardens."

"Was he tall or short? Dark haired or fair?" Dot asked.

"He was a good bit taller than the murdered girl, and I'm not certain about the hair, seeing as he was wearing a hat, but I feel like it was dark 'cause I remember thinking the pretty little blonde had a dark-haired sweetheart."

"How far away would you say you were from them?" he asked.

"Quite a ways. Much farther than from here to the far end of this street."

Dot nodded. "What was your impression of his clothing? Would you have said he was a gentleman?"

"Yes, I would. I remember as Mrs. Thorpe told me she worked at a gaming establishment where a lot wealthy men went, and I remembering thinking that she had likely met this man there."

Dot and Appleton exchanged grave gazes.

Mrs. Flint was not able to enlighten them any more. Before they left, he told the woman to keep his card and notify him if she remembered anything else.

They spent another hour on the street but learned nothing else.

* * *

Night had fallen by the time they were able to leave Lower Richard Street and climb into his carriage. "All right, Miss Dorothea Pankhurst. You appear to be having a difficult time suppressing your exuberance. Why have you been grinning so this past hour?" he asked.

She was fairly proud of herself that she had not

given in to the melancholy that had seized her since she'd read in the *Chronicle* about her fiancé's mistress. She had determined that, for now, she was going to push that to the back of her mind. And she had fairly well succeeded this afternoon.

Her mind was too occupied to fret over personal matters when there was a murderer lurking in their fair city.

And ever since they'd spoken with Mrs. Flint, she felt sure a picture of the murderer was emerging. "We may have no way of proving it, but I truly feel that Mrs. Flint saw the murderer."

"Come now, Dot. Can't a pretty girl meet a young man in the park?"

"I'm merely going by Miss Macintosh's past history. Do you not think it suspicious that she was seen conversing with a gentleman just before her death?"

He seemed to be weighing her words. "I suppose there's merit in what you say—but you are right. I doubt we'll ever know for sure."

"We finally do have *something* to go on, even if it's inconclusive!"

"You mean the fact the man is likely a gentleman?"

She nodded. "That and the fact he's possessed of dark hair and is above average height."

"That describes a great many men in Bath!"

"Except for the part about him being a gentleman."

"There is that." He was lost in contemplation for a moment. "If that is the case—that he's a gentleman—it almost certainly means that the man she met at Sydney Gardens is likely a patron of Mrs. Starr's."

"Exactly!"

"Seeing that I've spent the better part of my adult life at that establishment, I'm certain I am acquainted with every man who passes through Mrs. Starr's door."

Despite being in an enclosed carriage and wearing exceedingly warm clothing, a chill ran down her spine. That Forrester knew a murderer deeply disturbed her. "That's frightening."

"Better me than you or my sister."

It was statements like that which endeared him to her even more. She squeezed his arm in a display of affection. His hand settled on hers.

Chapter 12

That night when he and Annie collected Dot and her father, he thought his betrothed had never looked lovelier. She wore another new gown, and while he knew nothing about feminine fashions, he would say this sheer gown of pale blue appliquéd with lace and featuring short puffy sleeves had to be the epitome of what was fashionable.

He tried not to gawk at the way the dress dipped so low in the front and how enticingly plump her jiggly bits were. He forced himself to look away.

But he could not purge from his mind and body this overwhelming desire he had to take her in his arms and kiss her.

Such strong desire shocked him. In this week since Dot had consented to marry him, he hadn't thought about her in *that* way. Perhaps it was because he'd initially thought of her as that peculiar woman parading about Bath with those damn cats!

Once they arrived at the Upper Assembly Rooms, he urged Mr. Pankhurst and Annie to go ahead and save their chairs. "I need to have a private word with Dot in the Octagon."

As the others went on, she gave him a quizzing look. "Is anything amiss?"

He shook his head. "No. I just wanted to talk something over with you."

With ease that had come naturally to them, she slipped her arm through his, and he patted her hand in its long white opera glove as she gazed up at him.

"I have never before not been completely honest with Annie," he began. "You see, she is my favorite sister, and she and I have always been close."

Dot nodded sympathetically. "I see. It's bothering you that we are concealing this . . . this investigation from her?"

How was it that Dot always understood him so well? "Indeed it is."

"I understand. I didn't like not being forthright with her, either. She has become very dear to me. I think we need to take her into our confidence. Besides, three minds are better than two."

He lifted her hand and pressed a kiss into it. "Thank you."

"There's nothing to thank me for, you silly goose."

By the time they reached the assembly rooms, the dancing had commenced, and he tensed when he looked up and saw that Annie was dancing with Henry Wolf. Dot sat next to her father, but Appleton stayed standing while he glared at Wolf.

His group was soon joined by several members of the Blankenship family: Blanks and his wife Glee, along with Blanks' stepmother and his sister-in-law, Felicity Moreland and her husband, Thomas Moreland.

Appleton shook hands with Blanks and Moreland. "You fellows aren't playing cards?"

Blanks rolled his eyes. "The wives insist that we must dance with them first. Glee says people here will think she doesn't have a husband because I always abandon her in favor of the card room."

"As if she pines away unattended. . ." Appleton said playfully.

Blanks eyed his brother-in-law. "Moreland, I daresay, would rather dance attendance upon Felicity, but he's very accommodating to me. The best brother-in-law a fellow ever had."

Appleton did not doubt a word Blanks said. Moreland was besotted over his beautiful blonde wife, and when he wasn't here to lead her onto the dance floor, other men practically fought over that privilege.

"I understand felicitations are in order, Appleton," Moreland said, his gaze bouncing from him to Dot. "When's the wedding to occur?"

"We haven't set a date yet," Appleton said. "I have only known her for about two weeks."

Moreland smiled. "Love can be that way. I knew the moment I met Felicity—even though I was at death's door—I knew I'd never love another woman."

It was as if something inside Appleton caved in. If only he felt that way toward Dot. He forced a smile. "You certainly have been fortunate."

"Not *that* fortunate. You forget Felicity was married before me. I didn't think I'd ever have a prayer . . ."

"But now, old fellow," Blanks said in a reassuring voice, "you've got the love of your life *and* two very fine sons. What more could a man want?"

They both seemed so happy in matrimony. And Appleton felt so damned gloomy.

When the dance finally ended and Wolf returned Annie, Appleton directed his sternest glare at him.

Wolf did not linger.

The next dance was a waltz, and for some unaccountable reason, Appleton was happy to claim Dot for the shockingly intimate dance. The idea of those glorious breasts of hers pressed to his chest aroused him.

In the days since their betrothal, he'd not thought of her in the way a man thinks of a woman, not even when he'd asked her to marry him. It had been more like a business arrangement. As their hands clasped and their torsos came together in so intimate a fashion, he sorely regretted that he hadn't kissed her when she'd consented to marry him.

She must think him a foppy-boy!

As he glided along the ballroom with her in his arms, intoxicated by her sweet scent of spring roses, it occurred to him this was the woman who would bear his children. Thinking about her bearing his children got him to thinking about bedding her, and thinking about bedding her got him thinking about what it would be like to lie with her and . . . kiss her. . . to feel her tongue touch his . . . to slowly peel the garments from her body and stroke her satiny skin . . . to fill his hand with the plumpness of her breast . . .

All these thoughts nearly debilitated him with powerful desire. He looked at her as he'd never looked at her before, with a burning hunger.

Something in the back of his lust-fogged brain told him this was good. Desire for Dot certainly trumped his former indifference. He'd been dreading marrying a woman he couldn't love. But marrying a woman he potently desired. . . now that was something to look forward to.

He drew her closer and spoke huskily. "We need to set a date."

"For what?"

How could she not be feeling what he was feeling, not be throbbing with desire, not be anxious to swiftly wed? "For our wedding."

"Before we catch the murderer?" He was crushed by her disinterest in their marriage. "My dear Dot, we may never catch the murderer."

She nodded most morosely.

He had thought she'd be anxious to marry him. Didn't all women crave being married?

Then it occurred to him that perhaps she did not love him. Perhaps she was merely marrying him for his title.

It had never occurred to him that she wouldn't be agog to wed him. The fact that she might not be in love with him left him feeling low.

When they returned to their chairs, the only ones seated were Mr. Pankhurst and the elder Mrs. Blankenship, who were locked in lively conversation.

"I wonder if Papa will ask Mrs. Blankenship to dance," Dot said.

"What about his leg? Or is it his foot?"

"It seems to vary." She had a distasteful look on her face. "But it seems to vanish in Mrs. Blankenship's presence."

As, indeed, it did. The very next set, Mr. Pankhurst led the lady out onto the dance floor.

Appleton turned to Dot. "Forgive me, my love, for not telling you how splendidly you waltz."

"It's my dancing master who's to be commended."

He ran a seductive finger along her nose. It was

a perfect nose. "You're too modest. You were wonderful."

As his friends, including the newly arrived Sir Elvin, closed around him, he watched with a mixture of pride and jealousy as Dot became a figure of other men's admiration.

Not once during the remainder of the night was he able to claim her for a dance, not even for the Sir Roger de Coverley that closed out the night.

He stood back sulking as she merrily danced with a fashionably dressed young gentleman who'd just come from London and appeared to be taken with his fiancée. When he heard Glee comment on what a fine-looking man was dancing with Dot, Appleton was overcome by the urge to spar with said man during his sparring session the following morning. He would take great pleasure in knocking him to the floor.

On the way home that night, Mr. Pankhurst was effusive in his praise of Mrs. Blankenship. "Did you not think she was the most handsome of the older women there tonight?"

"Undoubtedly," Dot said.

"She regrets that I've still not met her son," Mr. Pankhurst continued. "He's a scholar, you know."

"So I'd heard," she said. "As is Sir Elvin's twin brother. I should like to meet them both."

"As would I," her father concurred. "As I told the good lady. She promised that she would present me with a copy of her son's latest book."

"How delightful. Did you know, Papa, his bride helps him with his research?"

"I didn't, but Mrs. Blankenship did say they were both very bookish and not inclined to attend assemblies."

Mr. Pankhurst soon resurrected the topic of

Mrs. Blankenship. "And was Mrs. Blankenship not an excellent dancer?"

"Frightfully good," Annie answered. "But I was awfully impressed with your unfaltering

skill, Mr. Pankhurst. I cannot credit that it's been more than twenty years since you've danced."

He shrugged. "I suppose it's one of those skills that always comes back to one." When they reached Dot's house, Mr. Pankhurst left the coach first.

As Appleton moved toward the house, he slowed and whispered to Dot. "*As You Like It* is being performed at the theatre. I should like to take you tomorrow night."

Her eyes shimmered. "I should love to see a Shakespearean play above anything!"

He stopped halfway between his coach and her front door. "I can think of one more thing," he said in a low, husky voice, his head dipping as he drew her close. He'd intended to gently settle his lips on hers, but once he found the velvety warmth of her compliant mouth, he was powerless to tame his hungry yearning. He devoured her in the rhythm of the moist, spiraling intensity of the kiss.

He could have gone on endlessly, kissing a trail to her enticing breasts, but for the proximity to her father and his sister bringing him back to his senses. "Oh, my love, I am most eager to make you—and only you—my wife."

Still breathless, he stood back and regarded her. She was even more captivating than the Italian opera singer who'd so mesmerized him several years earlier. And this woman would soon be his.

Though she faced him, her dark lashes lowered,

hiding her reaction to their kiss. But she could not hide the fact she was as breathless as he.

When he returned to the coach, he was so stunned by the powerful effect of Dot's kiss he completely forgot that he was sharing the carriage with Annie. They were half way to their house when he remembered she sat across from him. Then he remembered he was out of charity with her. He glared. "I am unhappy that you've danced with Henry Wolf again."

"Really, Timothy. You're being quite the ogre. The man couldn't be nicer to me. And he's sinfully rich. I don't know why you dislike him so."

"I have my reasons. In the past, you've always trusted my judgment."

She stomped her slipper. "I think you're being an ogre."

Being head of the family was no easy task.

Chapter 13

"Where's Annie?" Dot asked as Forrester showed her into the coach the following night. Would this be the first time she would be alone with him at nighttime?

"She had promised to attend a musical with Sir Elvin's sister."

Dot frowned. "I shall miss her." As fond as she was of Annie, though, she didn't really mean it. Truth be told, Dot was thrilled to have Forrester all to herself, especially after the intoxicating intimacy of the kiss they had shared the previous night.

"You'll be seeing much of my sister the rest of your life. I, for one, am happy to be alone with my intended."

His statement delighted her. "We've been alone a good bit during our investigations."

He put an arm around her. He smelled of sandalwood, and she was acutely aware of his breathing—things she'd not noticed when they were accompanied in the carriage by her father or Annie.

"But it's different at night," he whispered hoarsely.

Her pulse accelerated. His tone was intimate. She was not accustomed to Forrester speaking in such a tender voice. She wondered if he were going to kiss her again. Even though nearly four-and-twenty hours had elapsed since that heavenly occurrence, its magical effect was as vivid now as when she'd felt the first brush of his lips on hers and had nearly unraveled.

How puzzled she'd been later in the dark comfort of her bedchamber. How could an action as simple as a kiss cause such an onslaught of passion? Every part of her, body and soul, reacted. And how could she have the clarity of thought at such an intoxicating moment to realize that her lover did *not* find her inept? She swelled with an airy sense of wellbeing at that discovery.

Soon the coach pulled up at the theatre.

She was unprepared for the grandeur of the Theatre Royal with its fancy gilded boxes climbing the wall. Red flocked paper with an Egyptian pattern covered the walls, and crimson curtains festooned with thick gold fringe hung at each box. She was even more joyful when she learned that the Appleton family had its own box.

They took their seats on the front row of the box where a shiny brass rail offered an extra protection against falling into the pit. The Appleton box had a prime view of the stage below.

"Will anyone be joining us?" she asked.

"No, it will just be the two of us. When my other sisters are in town, the box becomes overrun with them and their friends."

"A pity Papa didn't come with us. We could have asked the elder Mrs. Blankenship to share our box, too."

Forrester smiled. "That would undoubtedly have made your father happy."

"So his partiality toward the widow has not escaped your notice, either?"

He chuckled. "Hardly." He took her hand. "I want you all to myself."

She felt the same but was too proud or possibly too shy to admit it.

"Have you seen Shakespeare performed before?"

Her brows hiked. "What do you think?" She was attempting to act normal, though since their hands had clasped, her fluttering chest seemed to be expanding.

"I think it unlikely to have been performed in rural Lincolnshire."

"Clever man."

"And do you appreciate Shakespeare?"

"I do, and it's impossible for me to convey to you how greatly I'm looking forward to tonight's play."

Soon the candles were extinguished, and the curtain went up. Her breath caught over the rich silks of the Elizabethan costumes in bright reds and greens. She quickly became engrossed in the plot, in every nuance of the dialogue, in the sheer pleasure she received from watching this delightful comedy.

How happy she was that she would be marrying and settling in Bath where such delights as the theatre, musicals, and assemblies were held throughout the year. Even simple acts like walking from her house to Forrester's provided a diversity of people and conveyances and architecture like she'd never before known.

At the same time, it shamed her to admit she never again wanted to live at Blandings. She would miss the villagers and her family's servants she'd known all her life, but she would never miss the monotony of the days.

No wonder she'd become so attached to her cats! As much as she loved her kitties, she thought as she squeezed her betrothed's strong hand, they did not compare to people and would never be able to compete with the man she would marry. How strange it seemed that a month ago she knew not of his existence, and now the thought of not spending her life with him was unbearable. How could she have fallen in love so thoroughly in so short a time?

During the intermission after the third act, Glee Blankenship and her mother-in-law came to their box. "And where is your dear father?" the elder Mrs. Blankenship asked as she came to sit on the other side of Dot.

Dot felt guilty she'd not even thought to ask her father. How he would have welcomed the opportunity to see Mrs. Blankenship. "Knowing that my Papa is no great fan of the bard, I neglected to invite him." That much was true.

"Typical man," Mrs. Blankenship said. "I suppose he'd rather be playing whist."

That gave Dot an idea. She nodded. "I should love to have a gathering at our house that would indulge my father's interest in whist. Do you play?" she asked the older woman.

"I adore whist, and I should welcome any invitation that would include me in an evening of whist, especially with your delightful father."

That Mrs. Blankenship obviously returned Mr. Pankhurst's affection pleased Dot. Her own betrothal had presented the problem of leaving her father alone at Blandings, a most distasteful prospect. She would have been happy to have her father live with her and Forrester, but her father, quite naturally, preferred his own home, a home he was proud of and which had belonged to the Pankhurst family for well over two hundred years.

While the women chatted, Forrester rose and went to speak with Blanks, who'd come into the box after the women.

At the end of the intermission, the Blankenships returned to their own box.

When the play ended, Dot joined the audience in clapping heartily for the excellent cast. She turned to Forrester. "This has been wonderful! I shall never forget this night and seeing my first production of Shakespeare."

He lifted her hand and kissed it. "It's merely the first of many."

Outside, it had begun to rain. She was thankful they'd come in Forrester's coach and happy to see his coach awaiting. Inside the dark cubicle, he gathered her close. She could have sighed with deep contentment.

"I've spoken with Annie about the inquiries you and I have been making about Ellie Macintosh's murder," he said.

"Allow me to guess. She wishes to join us in our queries."

"Of course. You two think entirely too much alike."

"She *is* to be my sister."

He squeezed her hand. "Tomorrow the three of us will go speak with Ellie's friend Maryann. Sir Elvin found out for us where she lives and told her to be expecting a visit from me."

"She knows you?"

"Seeing that she works at Mrs. Starr's and seeing that I have been playing there since I came down from Oxford, yes."

They'd not gone far when he pressed a kiss

onto her cheek. She felt as if an explosion occurred inside her chest.

Is he going to kiss me again? Her heartbeat roared, and she was filled with trepidation, worried her inexperience could displease him, though he'd given every indication of complete satisfaction the previous night.

As the coach drew nearer to her street, her pulse hammered. Even though no words were spoken, she knew he was going to kiss her.

"Given the rain," he murmured, "I won't be able to give you a proper good-night kiss on your doorstep." His lips found hers in the dark. His arms closed around her, drawing her close.

She was swamped by unexpected emotions. This was no quick peck. It was as if his lips were an extension of hers. As his hands traced sensuous circles on her back, she was lost to the overwhelming pleasure of melding into one with this man she adored. Her ragged breath ebbed and surged like a raging sea.

Had he ever breathed so huskily before? Or was she just more aware because they were so close?

Her arms came fully around him as her breasts flattened against his chest. She experienced the urge to be as close to him as skin, his delicious sandalwood-scented skin.

She was vaguely aware that he must be as satisfied as she with this intimacy for he made no effort to stop, no effort to cease his little grunts of pleasure.

When his coach stopped in front of her house, she could have wept with disappointment. His head lifted, and he pressed soft kisses on her forehead, her cheeks, and—to her complete astonishment—on the tops of her breasts as his hand cupped their plumpness. Her cheeks flushed.

She'd never felt more womanly.

He walked with her to the front door, though she had implored him not to in the rain. They stood briefly just before her footman swept open the door. Forrester gently ran a finger lovingly down her nose, bent and kissed her on the cheek, then said his farewells as—soaked—he returned to his coach.

In her blissful stupor, she could have wafted up the staircase without her feet touching the steps. Though the man she loved had never proclaimed a deep affection for her, tonight's and last night's passionate kisses gave her hope.

* * *

Back in the coach, Appleton let out a huge sigh. Kissing Dot had been most pleasurable. Thank God that aspect of their marriage would answer well. He found her intoxicatingly desirable.

He'd only paid lackluster attention to tonight's play because he'd been so obsessed over Dot and the fact he was alone with her in the dark. Her low-cut gown had him throbbing with the desire to feel her, taste her, possess her.

The sooner they married, the sooner he could slake his hunger.

Still he could not dispel the notion that had come to him at the assembly, the notion that she might not be in love with him. He could not deny that her response to his greedy kiss tonight was warm enough. There was nothing cold about her. But, then, Dot *was* possessed of an affectionate nature.

He had only to remember the way she used to tote those damned cats about the city, to visualize the way she caressed the damned things to be reminded of her affectionate nature. Then, too, there was the way her heart had gone out to Ellie's memory, even though she'd never met her.

Was her generous spirit the reason she kissed so satisfyingly? He wished he could believe she was in love with him—a selfish sentiment, given that he was not in love with her.

Chapter 14

"Sir Elvin told Ellie's friend to expect us today," Forrester said as the three of them strolled along the pavement in the direction of the city center. "Her lodgings are above a shop on Milsom Street."

"What's the lady's name?" Annie asked.

"Maryann. I forgot to ask what her surname is," Forrester said.

"Does Sir Elvin know why you wished to speak with Maryann?" Annie inquired.

He nodded. "Sir Elvin's the only other person with whom I've shared that we're making inquiries."

"Because you needed his assistance."

"Precisely."

Dot's stomach roiled when she thought of Forrester lying with his mistress after the play last night. "Did you go with Sir Elvin later last night?"

He shook his head.

So he was not going to tell her where he was. At least he wasn't going to lie.

"What did you do when you got home?" he asked.

"Papa and I played chess, and of course, the kitties vied for places on my lap. It got rather lively. Lover Boy and Nellie got into an altercation."

He quirked a brow. "Was either injured?"

Why was it the thought of violent actions aroused men's interest? "There's always a bit of blood drawn, and bits of fur go flying, but nothing serious. We've become accustomed to it with cats. They're not as docile with one another as dogs." She looked up at him. "I daresay like most men, you prefer dogs."

"I do—but that's not to say I have anything against cats."

It did not escape Dot's notice that Annie looked askance at him over that last comment.

When they reached Milsom the crowds on the pavement thickened. By walking closest to the street, Forrester's body served to shield the ladies' gowns from splatters.

"Who won the chess game?" he asked.

Dot's brows shot up. "Would you care to guess?"

"If I were still a wagering man—which I'm not—my money would be on you."

She wondered if he were telling her the truth about not gambling any more, or was it a ploy to get his hands on her fortune? After all, he was a noted profligate, according to the *Bath Chronicle*.

She eked out a smile. "You'd be right, sir."

"Why so formal?"

"In case you haven't noticed, there is a disparity in our stations."

"Not after we're wed. You'll be the same rank as me, Lady Appleton-to-Be."

It was difficult to remain out of charity with him. She had only to think of herself as his wife—she didn't give a fig that he was a viscount—to forget to be wounded.

And she had only to remember being held in his powerful arms the night before, being thoroughly kissed by him. She could have sighed out loud.

Before a wedding could occur, though, she had to talk to him and make it clear she would not tolerate infidelity in a marriage. She'd heard that's how marriages in the *ton* were conducted, and if it were so, she wanted no part of it—even if she had to leave Forrester and return to Blandings.

"What shop are we looking for?" she asked.

"A draper's by the name of Foley's."

"I know it," Annie said.

Dot nodded. "Me, too. I remember it's on the other side of the street."

Annie smiled. "That's right."

"I've lived in Bath for years and never noticed it, and how long have you been here?" he asked Dot.

She shrugged. "About five weeks."

"You're making me feel most inferior."

"Wait until you play chess with me," she said, giving him an exaggerated haughty grin.

"I shall have to abstain. My pride is already bruised."

She wondered why his pride would have been bruised. It certainly was not because he'd failed to notice a linen draper's.

At the next intersection, they had to wait for a pony cart laden with onions, a milk cart, several solo men on horses, and a mail coach to pass before the way was clear for them to cross the busy street.

Next to the door for Foley's Linen Drapers was another door leading to a steep flight of wooden stairs which they took to the landing on the third level, where there were two doors, one Number Four, the other Number Five. "She's at Four," he said as he knocked.

He knocked several times before a voice behind the door asked. "Who do you be?"

Dot didn't blame the girl for being cautious. After all, her closest friend had been brutally murdered.

"It's Lord Appleton."

The door opened, and a young woman—or was she still a girl?—smiled at him in obvious recognition. "Sir Elvin told me to expect you and yer lady friend today. Won't you come in? I'm sure yer lordship is accustomed to much finer lodgings than this, but I aim to keep it clean."

They swept into the shabby chamber. It was a fairly large room that served a trio of purposes. A lumpy bed edged into one corner and an eating table and chair into another while another third of the chamber accommodated a sofa covered in faded chintz. The clean wooden floors had no rugs, but simple cotton curtains covered the front and back windows.

The girl herself could not have reached twenty. Even though Maryann obviously could not afford costly clothing, she dressed stylishly in a mint green morning dress with puffed sleeves and scooped neckline. Her white, white skin resembled the finest porcelain, and her coppery hair coiled into ringlets.

It took no great understanding for Dot to realize Mrs. Starr shrewdly selected her girls because of their beauty, for Maryann's face and figure were both flawless.

Just being in her presence made Dot feel even more inadequate.

Forrester faced the girl. "I'm sorry I don't know your full name."

"It's Maryann Simpkins."

"Miss Simpkins, I should like to present you to my sister, Annie Appleton, and my betrothed, Miss Pankhurst."

Maryann dipped into a curtsy to each.

Not wanting to feel superior to the girl, Dot returned the curtsy. "It's a pleasure to meet you."

Maryann waved toward the sofa. "Won't you please sit?"

Dot and Annie sat down, but Forrester chose to remain standing.

"It may seem odd that we're calling on you today," Forrester said, "but both Miss Pankhurst and I are grievously affected over the tragic death of your friend Ellie Macintosh, and we wish to do everything in our power to learn the identity of the fiend responsible for her murder . . ."

"And make sure he's punished," Dot added.

The lady's eyes filled with tears. "I can't get it out of my mind. I was with her just the afternoon she died. Who knew I'd never see her again? Who could have known a monster would deprive her of life?" A sob burst from her, but she quickly recovered. "For all I know, he could come for me next."

"That's another reason I'm so determined to find the madman," he said. "We can't allow him to slay again. Perhaps you know something that will help us find him."

She shook her head. "I don't know nothing."

"Did Miss Macintosh speak to you of coming into some money recently?" Dot asked, her voice gentle.

Maryann's eyes widened. "She did. That last afternoon."

"How did she get it?" Forrester asked.

"That she wouldn't say. All I know is that she

did something she was sorry she'd done."

"Would you say she was melancholy that afternoon?" Dot asked.

"She was. She was being very hard on herself. She kept saying it was too late to give the money back. Her wicked deed had been done."

"But you don't know what the wicked deed was?" he asked.

"No idea," Maryann said.

"Do you know if there was a man she saw? A sweetheart?" Dot asked.

Maryann shook her head. "I never knew her to ever give encouragement to any man. She thought they were all interested in . . . well, in something she wasn't. Ellie was a country girl at heart. She'd like to have married a farm laborer and settled on land and had a family, but I got the feeling she felt there was no place where she belonged, though Ellie was very tight-lipped. She didn't talk much about herself."

"Did you ever see her speaking with any men outside of Mrs. Starr's?" he asked.

She pondered this for a moment. "No, never. I'm sorry I'm not of any help."

"It's not your fault," Dot said, standing. "But we're not going to give up."

When they reached her door, Maryann said, "Wait!"

They whirled around to face her.

"I just remembered something, something I believe is very important. She was going to come into some money that same night as she died. She must have been planning to meet a man."

"The killer," Dot murmured, a chill spiking along her spine.

"And you have no idea who she was going to

meet?" he asked.

Maryann shook her head morosely. "She said she hoped she wouldn't be late for w-w-work." Maryann burst out crying. "Sh-sh-she never made it to work that night."

Forrester moved to her and settled a gentle hand on her shoulder. "Thank you for talking with us today. If I can ever be of assistance, you can find me at Camden Place. And I beg of you, do not walk alone at night and always lock your door."

"Thank you, my lord. As it is, Mrs. Starr has retained the services of a hackney coach to take home all the girls at the end of the evening. All the girls that's left, that is."

"That's very good of her."

Dot came and set a hand on her forearm. "If you remember anything else, do let Lord Appleton know. Do give the lady your card, my darling," Dot said to Forrester.

It took him a moment to find which pocket he'd put the cards in. "We shan't rest until the wicked man pays for his crime," he said as they left.

* * *

Now they had gotten information, such as it was, from Ellie's landlady and elderly neighbor as well as Ellie's closest friend, Appleton knew barely more than he'd known before he started. He felt like the exhausted fisherman with empty nets.

They had learned Ellie had taken money for doing something she regretted, and that she had met with a possibly dark-haired gentleman of above average height at Sydney Gardens. It took no great intelligence to believe the two things they'd learned were related.

Seeing the fear that petrified the youthful

Maryann made him even more determined to do everything in his power to stop the murderer from striking again.

Girls like Maryann and Ellie didn't deserve to die. They were young and harmless and without protectors. They should have many more years to look forward to, years that would see them marry and have families of their own.

"You're being awfully quiet," Dot said as they walked along Bath's stone pavement. "Reflecting?"

He nodded. "Did you see the terror on her face?"

"It was heart wrenching," Dot said. "I'm so grateful not to live alone."

Even though they were going uphill, Dot did not seem to have any problem matching him step for step. Annie was accustomed to it, but few London-bred ladies could tolerate this city's hilly terrain. "You are accustomed to walking when you're back in Lincolnshire?" he asked.

"I am. I've always preferred it to riding. I daresay you will not be surprised to learn that my father prefers riding. I find that always riding can make one lazy as well as corpulent."

He couldn't help himself. His gaze traveled over her pleasing figure. "I am happy you prefer walking to riding."

"What you really mean is that you're happy I'm not corpulent!"

"My brother has little practice speaking to respectable young ladies," Annie said, shooting him a mischievous stare.

He glared at her. Were she younger, she deserved a good spanking.

As they walked along, he thought of how much his sisters disliked walking at their country estate, complaining about muddying their shoes and the hemlines of their dresses. Each of them preferred riding horses, and their very favorite mode of transport was being ensconced in a warm carriage. Dot was a most singular lady, to be sure.

And such an affectionate nature! He'd regretted allowing Annie to accompany them today. He rather looked forward to capturing another kiss from the woman he was going to marry.

Ah, marriage! For the first time, he found himself looking forward to marrying Dot . . . and sharing her bed.

Chapter 15

Early the following afternoon, the elder Mrs. Blankenship presented herself and her grandchildren at the Pankhurst residence, where the man of the house was delighted over the surprise visit.

"I've brought you a copy of my son's book," she said, placing the leather-bound volume in his hands.

His face brightened even more as he examined the title: *Observations on a Parliamentary Government*. "I shall begin reading it this very day." He met her proud gaze. "It was very thoughtful of you, my dear Mrs. Blankenship."

"Have the children come to play with the kitties?" Dot asked.

"If it's not inconvenient for you."

"Not in the least."

This time Baby Gregory was not content to sit upon the sofa and have a docile cat placed in his lap. He took to chasing Lover Boy, the largest of Dot's felines. When the cat politely allowed the toddler to catch up with him, Gregory almost took Dot's breath away when he promptly straddled the cat in an attempt to ride him as if he were a pony.

Before Dot could be struck with apoplexy, Mrs. Blankenship snatched up the errant little lad. "No, no."

Dot exhaled.

The grandmother then had her grandson return to the sofa whereupon Dot placed Preenie Queenie on his lap. To Dot's delight, Preenie—the most indolent of her cats—was content to sit and allow the little lad to stroke her mass of fluffy fur.

"I've come to tell you," Mrs. Blankenship said to Dot, "that I've spoken with my son, and he's agreed to participate in your salon. He's even coaxed his good friend Melvin Steffington to come. All you have to do is set the date."

Dot eyed her father. "What do you think, Papa?"

"You're to make all decisions regarding hostess matters."

"Then I'd like to set it for Friday."

"That should give you enough time to invite everyone," Mrs. Blankenship said.

"Tell me," Dot's father said to their visitor, "how does one differentiate among the three Mrs. Blankenships?"

"An excellent question," that lady said. "We are referred to by our husbands' first name. Therefore, Glee is referred to as Mrs. Gregory, and my daughter-in-law as Mrs. Jonathan, and I'm known as Mrs. James, my late husband's name."

Dot could not see her father addressing the lady by her dead husband's name. He was probably angling to be able to call her by her Christian name.

Preenie Queenie suddenly stood on all four legs and leapt away from Baby Gregory, who began to cry as he waved an index finger at the fleeing cat. Dot quickly snagged Lover Boy to replace Preenie, but she sat on the other side of the wee lad with a firm hand on the cat's back to discourage him from taking flight.

Meanwhile, the perpetually-talking Joy had hiked Fur Blossom over her tiny shoulder and patted at her as if she were a real babe. Dot was shocked that Fur Blossom permitted it. "I believe Fur Blossom is vastly fond of you, Joy."

"I know. She loves me. I wish she had a baby cat so I could get her and take her home. My papa said I could have my very own kitty." She glared at her brother. "But I can't get one until Baby Gregory's big enough to have a doggie."

Why was it that men always had to have their dogs, Dot wondered.

She spent the duration of Mrs. James Blankenship's visit attempting to manage her cats with the two active children while her father and Mrs. James chatted like old friends.

When they left, Mr. Pankhurst walked them to the front door with nary a limp.

* * *

While Dot was adept at calling on pensioners of her father's or the sick in cottages scattered around the Lincolnshire countryside, she was embarrassed to admit she had no experience paying a morning call on society matrons. At the advanced age of three-and-twenty, she could hardly beg her father to accompany her in returning the visit Glee Blankenship had so kindly paid to the Pankhursts. She had considered asking Annie to come with her, but she abandoned the scheme. If she were going to be the Viscountess Appleton, she needed to learn how to go about in society. By herself.

She rather tortured herself wondering if she should first send along a note telling the hostess to expect her call but remembered that Mrs.

Gregory Blankenship and her sister had just popped in at the Pankhurst residence, as had Mrs. James Blankenship.

When Dot and her father had first arrived in Bath, he had seen to it that she had cards printed up with their Bath address upon them. "A proper lady will need these," he'd told her. She had not needed them up to this point, but she had observed that callers at her house had presented their cards to Topham, who in turn used them in announcing the visitors to his masters. Mr. Pankhurst had told her the cards were also left when the hostesses were out to allow them to know who had called.

Therefore, after an inordinate amount of time spent on her toilette and having Meg assist her into a rose-coloured muslin she knew to be exquisite, Dot stuffed her reticule with new cards and began to walk to Queen Square.

She wasn't sure she wanted Glee Blankenship to even be home because she wasn't confident she knew the proper procedure for paying a morning call. But she did know that good manners demanded she return the call Glee had been so thoughtful to pay. She had another reason for calling today. She wanted to invite Glee to the Pankhurst salon on Friday.

As she drew near Queen Square, she found herself hoping Glee wasn't at home. She would just leave a card, go on her carefree way, and would have fulfilled the social obligation.

Glee Blankenship was at home, and her drawing room was fairly bulging with callers, some of whom Dot knew and some who were complete strangers.

Glee and her sister, Felicity Moreland, greeted

her warmly, as did Mrs. James Blankenship. "My dear Miss Pankhurst, I don't think you've met my daughter-in-law Mary Blankenship," the elder Mrs. Blankenship said. She indicated a plain, dark-haired woman who sat next to her. "She's married to my son Jonathan. They're practically newlyweds."

"It's been nearly two years now, Mother," the plain Mrs. Blankenship said.

Dot perked up. "Your husband's the scholar! My Papa was reading your husband's book when I left the house."

The young wife looked pleased. "That's gratifying—and I suppose my husband is a scholar to a certain degree." She glanced at an exceptionally pretty blonde woman. "Though Mrs. Steffington's husband is the true scholar."

"Your husband's Sir Elvin's twin!" Dot said to the blonde.

The lovely woman nodded. "You've met Sir Elvin?"

Glee answered instead of Dot. "Of course she has! She's to marry his best friend." Mrs. Steffington's eyes rounded. "Oh, you're the . . . the one who's to marry Lord Appleton."

Dot was almost certain she was about to say *the heiress*. Did everyone in Bath know Forrester was marrying the daughter of a very wealthy man?

"Forgive me for not making better introductions," Glee said. She proceeded to properly introduce Dot to the assembled ladies.

"So does your husband look exactly like his twin?" Dot asked Catherine Steffington.

"That's what everyone says. I, too, thought so until I . . . fell in love with Melvin. Now I could never, ever get them mixed up."

"I must confess," Dot said, "I cannot wait to meet Bath's resident scholars. Coming from so rural an area, it's thrilling for me to think I'll have the opportunity to meet someone who's published a book. Please thank your husband for agreeing to come to our salon Friday night."

"I'm greatly looking forward to it," Mrs. Steffington said.

Dot addressed Glee. "I wanted to personally invite you to the salon, and it looks as if I'm going to have the opportunity to invite your sister and the others all at once."

"I will own," Catherine Steffington said, "I was surprised when Melvin told me he had agreed to read from his work at your salon, Miss Pankhurst. My husband normally lacks social instincts."

"Is that why I haven't seen you at assemblies?" Dot asked the pretty blonde.

Catherine Steffington nodded. "Melvin abhors dancing."

The younger Mrs. Blankenship concurred. "Jonathan's not fond of assemblies, either."

Glee directed her attention to Dot. "Mary was my school friend long before she ever met and fell in love with Jonathan, and I can vouch for the fact she, too, was not enamored of assemblies."

"How fortuitous that your old friend has become your sister," Dot said.

"It is indeed," the quieter Mary Blankenship said. "I was an only child."

"It's the same with me," Dot said.

Glee turned to her sister-in-law. "And, like you, Mary, Miss Pankhurst has already become quite close to Annie Appleton."

"Indeed I have. Since coming to Bath my good

fortune knows no bounds."

"Lord Appleton, I am sure, will make a wonderful husband," Mrs. Steffington said.

Such a comment gladdened Dot. "It strikes me," she said, regarding Mrs. Steffington, "that your husband and Sir Elvin are vastly different."

Every person in the chamber broke into laughter. Catherine Steffington laughed so hard tears streamed from her huge blue eyes. "The twins are as dissimilar as a tortoise to a hare."

"And I daresay your bookish husband is the tortoise," Glee said.

Catherine Steffington nodded. "Indeed, the scholarly tortoise."

"I think Miss Pankhurst's idea of a literary salon sounds delightful," Mrs. Moreland said. "I'm sure Thomas will enjoy it."

"My son's not nearly as shy as Mr. Steffington," Mrs. James Blankenship said. "I do believe Jonathan might even enjoy reading from his works in front of a room full of admiring friends."

Dot no longer felt out of place. Every woman here made her feel welcome.

Then the butler entered the chamber and handed Glee three cards at once. "How exciting! All the Appleton sisters have come. That must mean Agnes and Abby are back in Bath."

Just when Dot was getting comfortable. What would Forrester's other sisters think of her? Would they be as gracious as Annie?

Her pride was minimally bruised. They'd come to see Glee Blankenship instead of her. And she was soon to be a member of their family.

Her insides fluttered as she watched the doorway. Annie came in first. The second sister looked remarkably like Annie, and of course, they both looked remarkably like Forrester. The third one, though, looked vastly different. She was short and plumper and was possessed of blonde hair. Dot immediately thought of Mrs. Steffington's comment about the twin brothers being as dissimilar as a tortoise to a hare. That's how the smaller sister looked compared to Annie and the other one.

Annie's face brightened when she saw Dot, and she came straight to her. "Your father told us you'd be here! I'm ecstatic that you will finally get to meet my gallivanting sisters—soon to be your sisters."

The one who looked so much like Annie was Agnes, and the short one, who was also the youngest, was Abby. Agnes not only resembled Annie, she adopted her mannerisms and was possessed of the same graciousness Annie always exhibited—without quite as much exuberance.

"Oh, I declare," Abby exclaimed upon being introduced to Dot, "she's much prettier than . . ." She paused for a moment, embarrassed, then recovered and said, "than the women who normally appeal to Timothy!"

Dot could feel the heat climbing up her face. The sisters must have been told—possibly in a letter?—about Dot's plainness. Thank God her father had averted even more painful humiliation by indulging her with a fine wardrobe and a talented maid to dress her unruly hair.

Still, she felt awkward—even humiliated. Either Forrester or Annie—both of whom she had come to love—must have written about her to their sisters. And what they'd written could not have been flattering.

"That's a positively wretched thing to say about

our brother," Annie scolded her younger sister. "We hardly know what kinds of women he's been attracted to since he's never before deigned to bestow his affections on one. I'm exceedingly proud of the choice he's made in Miss Pankhurst."

"But what about Mrs. . ." Abby began but was cut off by a vicious glare from her eldest sister.

"And how, Miss Pankhurst, did you come by the name Dot?" Agnes asked in a smooth attempt to divert attention from the taboo subject of Forrester's mistress.

Dot could see that the gracious Agnes was like Annie in every way. "It's actually a shortened form of my given name, Dorothea." Even her voice trembled. She found herself wanting to cry and desperately trying not to.

"I should have known." Agnes directed a warm smile on Dot.

"Did you bring your cats today?" Abby asked. "How fortunate you are to possess several."

More crimson rose to Dot's face. Had everyone in Bath found her to be a laughing stock? Had Forrester or Annie written with amusement about the crazed newcomer who paraded about the city with her coddled felines?

Now that he had united himself with Dot, did her humiliation extend to Forrester?

How she wished she'd never come here today, never subjected herself to such continued humiliation. If she had never come to Bath, never met Forrester, never strung up herself for ridicule and heartache, she wouldn't be suffering as she was now. Her life had been so much simpler, so much more comforting back at Blandings.

She couldn't be angry with Forrester's youngest sister. She was only voicing what she'd heard about Dot.

All Dot could think of was her powerful desire to race home and weep, away from these pitying glances. She could only barely manage to respond to Abby. "My cats are at home, but you're welcome to come and meet them. I have four."

Abby's youthful face brightened. "That would be delightful."

"My sisters will come to know you and adore you as much as I," Annie said to Dot.

"Thank you." Dot got to her feet. "I must be going now, but before I do I should like to invite everyone in this chamber to come to our house on Friday night for the salon to feature our two scholars, Jonathan Blankenship and Melvin Steffington."

Annie stood also and turned to the hostess. "I must go as well. I particularly need to speak with Dot, but my sisters will stay." She glared at her youngest sister.

Dot had not wanted to be with anyone, but the last thing she wanted was to make a scene, especially after reminding everyone of how unfit she was to be in their society. She was even more unfit to be Viscountess Appleton.

Outside, Annie fell into step beside Dot, who was speeding along at a brisk pace. "I must apologize for Abigail. We cannot blame her thoughtless tongue on her youth. She's always been thoughtless and always a source of consternation to our family. I daresay ten years hence we'll still be apologizing to those whom she's not already alienated. I cannot tell you how unimaginably improper it was for her to allude to Timothy's mistress in such a setting. The girl wants for a brain."

It was impossible for Dot to withhold her tears any longer. She made not a whimper as they slid down her cheeks.

"Oh, Dot, dearest, dearest Dot. I am so sorry for Abby's foolish words."

"I have been the object of ridicule, have I not?"

Annie did not respond.

Her silence hurt more than confirmation. For Annie was too much like Forrester. She could not lie.

Now Dot wept in earnest as she angrily strode toward the Circus, nearly blinded by the onslaught of her own tears.

"I am so sorry. It was just that you *were* different. But once we came to know you, we both came to care deeply for you."

Dot stopped, swiped away her tears, and faced Annie. "He knew about my dowry, did he not?"

Annie shrugged. "How am I to know what knowledge my brother possessed?"

Again, Annie could not tell an outright lie.

But she had unmistakably answered Dot's question.

Chapter 16

Though his sisters seldom came into Appleton's domain—the wood-paneled library at the rear of the townhouse's ground floor—Annie awaited him in the dimly lit room. He could tell by the troubled look on her face that something was wrong.

He fleetingly wondered if the interview with Ellie's friend had disturbed her. That a murderer was still loose in their city was enough to terrify any woman.

"What's wrong?" He moved to her.

She sighed. "Abby's returned, and so has her careless tongue. She's offended Dot to the point I wouldn't be surprised if she wishes to break your betrothal."

He felt as if a cannonball had slammed into him. His first reaction was not disappointment over the withdrawal of the huge dowry he so desperately needed. It was the crushing intelligence that his youngest sister had hurt Dot.

Dot was perhaps the most genuinely caring person he'd ever known. There was little on earth he wouldn't endure to spare her. His eyes narrowed to slits. "What did Abby say?"

Annie rolled her eyes. "What didn't she say? And in so public a forum!"

His gut clinched. "Where?"
"In the absolute crush that was Glee

Blankenship's drawing room. I declare, there wasn't an empty chair!"

He winced. He knew nothing disparaging about Glee or her sister, but the urge to spread gossip typically ran strong among the female gender. "What did The Pest say?" He dreaded hearing the truth.

"Allow me to say her allusion to your mistress was the most harmless intelligence she conveyed."

He closed his eyes and cursed. "And the harmful?"

Annie shook her head sadly. "Oh, Timothy, it was ghastly! When Abby was introduced to Dot she all but said she had expected Dot to be ugly."

He cursed again.

"Dot's intelligent enough to know that any information about her had originated from either you or me."

He nodded, a sick feeling slamming into him. "I may have spoken of Dot in the most unflattering terms when we first met her." He drew a deep breath. "It's so contrary to what I now feel, I'd almost forgotten. Is there more?"

"Abby immediately asked about Dot's cats."

He sighed. "So either you or I must have written the girls about Dot's . . . peculiarities."

She nodded. "It was abundantly obvious Dot was embarrassed. And hurt."

"These are not insurmountable problems. Surely Dot realizes you and I have both grown to care very deeply for her."

"There's more."

He waited a moment while his sister gathered her wits about her enough to continue, and when she spoke, there were tears in her eyes. "Dot was understandably upset and was the first to leave. I followed." Annie swallowed hard. "She. . . she asked me if you had known about her fortune before you asked her to become your wife."

This time he cursed aloud. "So she thinks I'm a blasted fortune hunter who ridicules her behind her back?"

"I'm afraid so."

Neither spoke for several moments.

As angry as he was with his youngest sister, he was angrier with himself. Abby hadn't lied. All her thoughtless comments had been instigated by him before he had come to know and to care for Dot. "I must go to her now." He went to turn, but Annie caught his arm.

"I would advise against it. She was weeping. She'll be in a vastly irritable mood and won't feel in the least charitable toward you. Let her cry it out tonight, then go to her tomorrow. I know you care for her. Let her know your true feelings."

"Very well." He went to his desk and penned a note to Dot.

My Dearest Dot,
Expect me to call at ten in the morning.
Yours,
Forrester

Since he'd inherited the title he had signed all correspondence and documents with the simple surname Appleton, as was customary for men of rank. But with Dot, he could not think of using anything other than her own special name for him.

Calling him Forrester was just another example of the ways in which the two of them had grown close. He had come to feel an intimate connection with her.

Especially since kissing her the past two nights. The very memory created a deep yearning.

He called for a footman and requested he deliver the message to Miss Pankhurst.

* * *

Dot had told neither her father nor her maid the real reason she remained in her bedchamber all night and refused dinner. She merely said she wasn't feeling well and did not wish to be disturbed. Which was true. She just neglected to inform them she suffered from a bruised heart more than a physical infirmity. When one was heartsick, though, one's whole body suffered. She *had* lost her appetite. Her churning stomach *did* feel as if she were unwell. And she *was* too miserable to sleep.

As hurt and humiliated as she was, she derived a modicum of comfort from the note Forrester sent. *Dearest.* Never had she needed to see such an endearment more than she did then.

In the morning her mood brightened, aided by the glow of sunshine flooding her bedchamber. She and Meg took extra time with her toilette, and she wore a new morning dress that Mrs. Gainsworth had delivered the previous day.

Dot knew it was becoming on her. She had come to learn from his reactions what Forrester admired. She was oddly pleased that his favorite dresses were those that displayed her ample bosom. He also showed a preference for dresses either of white or white background. She supposed the white accentuated her teeth, which she was gratified to admit were uncommonly white. Or did they just seem so because her complexion was darker than what was acceptable for upper class ladies?

Today's dress was another exceedingly thin sprigged muslin of pink roses on white. She had learned that the thinner the muslin, the heftier its price.

Meg had procured rouge which she sparingly patted on Dot's cheeks to make them appear pink. The result could not have been more natural looking. For the first time in memory, Dot was possessed of pink cheeks.

Once Lord Appleton was announced, she sucked in her breath, left her bedchamber, and descended the stairs to join her father and him in the drawing room. She arrived just in time to hear her father offer him a glass of brandy, which Forrester politely declined.

"Papa! Lord Appleton is sure to think you a sot! One does not drink brandy at ten in the morning!" A quick glance confirmed that her father was, indeed, drinking brandy.

Mr. Pankhurst sighed. "It helps to blunt the pain of my many infirmities."

Her eyes narrowed. "Taking the baths would be much preferred. Will you go today?"

"If it's what my daughter desires."

"That's what your daughter desires." She then turned to Forrester, who had stood when she entered the chamber.

"You look lovely this morning," said he.

"Thank you." She thought he would then sit back down, but he did not.

"I had hoped, especially since it's such a fine day, that you and I could go for a walk."

Her heartbeat pounded. She knew he would bring up the embarrassing topic which had so troubled her the previous day. But she also knew they had to discuss it.

Last night she had decided she might have to break their betrothal, though she wanted to marry Forrester more than she'd ever wanted anything. This walk with him could prove to be the most important in her entire three-and-twenty years.

Once they were on the pavement, he offered his arm, and she placed her hand on it, which he quickly covered with his. His lightest touch seemed to open up her body like a flower, creating a molten ache only he could heal.

Her thoughts spun to their last kiss, to the heat of his body pressed against hers, his mouth hot and wet and demanding, and all rational thought fled her need-fogged brain.

She was only vaguely aware of the passing horses and carts and equipages. She would have been incapable of describing a single person they passed as they trod along the busy street.

Finally he spoke. "I pray you slept better last night than I."

She did not respond. Pride prevented her from admitting her distress.

"My sister informed me that you were upset yesterday." He pressed her hand. "Nothing could make me more miserable that to think I could ever have hurt you." He stopped right there on the pavement and looked down at her.

Her heart leapt at the pain on his beloved face, at the dewy melancholy of his mossy eyes. "No woman exists whom I care for more deeply than I care for you, and that's the honest truth."

He might not have used the word *love*, but she knew it was as close as he could come.

And it was enough for her.

She could have sighed with relief. She would not have to break their engagement. "In addition to some of the comments made by your youngest sister," she began, but faltered when she realized they were blocking passage of others.

He nodded. "Come. We'll go to Crescent Field."

A few moments later they were on the massive lawn which swept into the shape of the Royal Crescent above it. They began to plod across it. "As I was saying, in addition to being distressed over some of the comments made by your sister Abby, there's another matter we must discuss before we can set a wedding date."

He raised a brow.

"Your mistress."

"That blasted Abby!"

They stood in the grass as she took both his hands. "My dearest Forrester, I've known about your Mrs. P for some time."

"That blasted *Bath Chronicle*!"

She nodded.

He bent forward and pressed a soft kiss to the tip of her nose. "That woman is history. As soon as you did me the honor of consenting to become my wife, I broke it off with her." He drew a breath. "Because you are to be my wife I will speak of something I would not normally discuss." He drew another breath. "My father kept mistresses. I did not approve. My mother was a wonderful woman, a devoted wife. She deserved my father's complete fidelity." He took her hands and kissed them. "I vow to you I will be a faithful husband."

She could ask for nothing more than the words he'd said to her today.

She had thought to ask him when he'd learned she was considered an heiress, but she didn't want to hear the truth.

For she already knew it.

* * *

When they returned to her house, Appleton joined her in the library where he helped her on the invitations to Friday night's salon. "You've been so helpful in assisting me with the list of invitees and providing their addresses," she said. "You don't have to stay. I can finish them and have them delivered this afternoon."

"I'll stay." Was it a weakness to admit he enjoyed being with her? There was also another matter they must decide.

It had already been more than two weeks since that damned Wolf had acquired his gambling debts. He had less than two weeks in which to get the money to save the house and keep that man from trying to marry Annie. Appleton needed to marry Dot soon. Her father had already agreed to present him the dowry upon their marriage.

"I'm desperate to marry you." He moved closer and pressed whispery kisses on the silky skin of her neck as he murmured. "I'm hungry to make you my wife." He emitted a low groan. "In every way."

She set down her pen and looked up at him with those big chocolaty eyes, and he thought he'd never seen a more desirable woman. When her hand stroked his thigh, he thought he could go mad with desire. "I must get a special license," he ground out.

Tracing sultry circles on his thigh, she nodded. "You can set the date," she said breathlessly.

He snatched her hand and kissed it. Otherwise he might have tried to ravish her on the floor of her father's library. He did not know what had gotten into him. No woman had ever aroused him as she did. "Then we'll marry before the week's out, my beloved."

With those words, he stood. By God, he was going to find a clergyman and get a special license immediately.

Chapter 17

Judging from the attendance, Dot would say her salon was a great success. Every person she had invited came. Once they had all arrived, Forrester took her hand and went to stand in front of the fireplace, the focal point at which the drawing room.

After he thanked everyone for coming, he made an announcement: "My dear Miss Pankhurst and I wish to tell those of you who have gathered here tonight that we're to marry on Wednesday morning in Bath Cathedral, and all of you . . ." Forrester scanned the assemblage, "my closest friends, are invited."

His comment was met with broad smiles, and Mrs. James Blankenship, who'd managed to seat herself next to Mr. Pankhurst, even clapped her hands to demonstrate her hearty approval.

"One other announcement: after tonight's discussions, whist tables will be set up for all who desire to play. Now," he said, "I'm going to step aside and allow our hostess to introduce our first speaker."

Dot had decided that even though she'd been told Melvin Steffington was the shyer of the two scholars, she would have him go first. Her reasoning was that his topic of a Roman philosopher/orator would be less appealing than

Jonathan Blankenship speaking on contemporary matters of politics. Having Jonathan go last would extend the discussions to enable all attendees who desired to further address the topic.

"It is my honor tonight," she began, "to present our first speaker whose newest work is a translation of some of Cicero's more obscure letters." She eyed Melvin, who looked so much like Sir Elvin she would not have been able to tell which was which were he not seated next to his pretty blonde wife. "Please welcome Dr. Melvin Steffington."

He slowly came to replace Dot in front of the fireplace and cleared his throat. "I have decided that instead of reading from my work tonight—which my wife tells me might be considered by some to be dull—I will tell you a little about the remarkable Roman who, in my opinion, came to personify the entire Renaissance movement to bring us out of the dark ages."

He went on to commend Cicero and explain that he gave up his life to defend his principles.

When Mr. Steffington finished, he asked for questions.

Abby Appleton's arm shot up, and he called upon her. Dot shuddered, hoping the unthinking young lady would not say something offensive to the shy scholar. Dot's glance met Forrester's. He looked anxious.

"I suppose, Mr. Steffington," Abby began, "that Cicero wrote in Latin?"

He nodded. "That is correct."

Abby shrugged. "I fail to understand why people like you continue to study Latin. We all know it's a dead language."

Dot and Forrester looked at one another, and

he rolled his eyes with exasperation.

Melvin Steffington did not answer for a moment. It was clear to Dot that he'd not anticipated questions of so naïve a nature. "Well . . . first, allow me to explain that Latin has heavily influenced every language spoken in Europe today, so I believe an understanding of Latin broadens one's vocabulary. But most importantly, these brilliant men who ruled the world's most civilized country almost two thousand years ago imparted significant wisdom which will benefit all mankind for the next two thousand years, and reading their works in the language in which they spoke is the purest, most exacting way to convey their thoughts and to fully understand them."

Dot was most relieved by Mr. Steffington's intelligent response—and thankful that Abby's careless words must not have offended him too badly.

"Well said," Forrester praised.

The gentlemen in the chamber continued to speak of Cicero, but the ladies, owing to their lack of a classical education, contributed little.

After a while Dot returned to the fireplace and addressed the gathering. "Thank you so much, Mr. Steffington, for such an enlightening discussion. I, for one, will be reading all the *translations* of Cicero that I can get my hands on—that is, after I read yours. He sounds like a brilliant, fascinating man, and we are indebted to you for sharing your wealth of research with us."

Then she proceeded to introduce Jonathan Blankenship. "Many of you know the younger Mr. Blankenship from his essays on political economy which appear regularly in the *Edinburgh Review*, and it is my privilege tonight to introduce Mr.

Jonathan Blankenship."

He came to take her place in front of those assembled. "Tonight I have decided to give all of you a preview of my article that will appear next month in the *Edinburgh Review*. I'll be promulgating penal reform."

Abby shrieked and covered her ears. "In front of ladies?"

Forrester issued an impatient oath. "I beg your pardon, Jonathan, but obviously my youngest sister is unacquainted with the word *penal*. Would you mind explaining it for her sake?"

Dot admired Forrester. What a good head of the family he made. How quick he was to analyze something. He would be an admirable husband.

Blanks and Sir Elvin could not hold back their laughter.

Jonathan quickly recovered. "Penal refers to punishment, particularly as it refers to incarceration and transportation. I will specifically be speaking to the need for a system of classifying crimes –and subsequent punishment—according to the severity of the crime."

Several heads nodded in agreement.

"For example," he said, "in Britain we have many, many minor crimes, such as poaching, that are punishable by death. It is my belief that the death penalty be reserved for crimes of murder. Lesser crimes should have lesser penalties."

More heads nodded.

He gave a clearly defined talk that laid out the problems that needed to be addressed, and he proposed solutions. When he finished, everyone in the chamber clapped, and a lively discussion ensued.

Topham began to circulate throughout the

chamber with a tray filled with glasses of port.

Dot was pleased when her guests got up and began to mingle while the footmen set up card tables.

Blanks came up to her. She was struck again by his handsomeness. He was the tallest man in the chamber and was possessed of thick hair in a rich dark brown and an exceedingly agreeable face that evoked a good nature. "You have caused considerable consternation in our house, Miss Pankhurst."

"How so?"

"Ever since my daughter has become acquainted with your cats, she gives me not a moment's peace. She's forever begging to have her own."

Dot laughed. "I am surprised you've not given in to her. I had been told—"

"You'd heard that it was impossible for me to deny the little minx anything?"

"Indeed."

He nodded remorsefully. "It's true. She and her mother both have a talent for bending me to their will."

"I understand you and your wife have known each other most of your lives."

"True."

"So you were always in love with one another?" Goodness, what had made Dot speak of so personal a matter?

He shrugged. "To be honest, I wanted no part of marriage. Glee tricked me into marrying her." He paused. "Once we were married—and completely against my own wishes—I became utterly obsessed with that little vixen I wed."

"That tells me that the marriage merely

affirmed the love you two always had for one another." Exactly what she was hoping for in her own forthcoming marriage.

"That's an intelligent observation, Miss Pankhurst. Allow me to say I hope you and Appleton are as happy as Glee and I."

Forrester came up and settled a hand at her waist. If a body could smile, hers would at this moment.

"And," Blanks said to her, "it looks as if I'm going to have to procure *two* cats. Much to my chagrin, Gregory has also become enamored of the creatures, even though I've always felt men—and boys—should have dogs."

"I am most happy to hear that," Dot said, then looked up at Forrester.

"I refuse to comment," her betrothed said.

Appleton and Blanks started talking, and she moved to Mrs. Steffington. "I am so gratified you persuaded your husband to be our featured guest tonight," Dot said. "He was most fascinating."

That lady beamed. "I agree, but I am a bit prejudiced."

"I am told your husband always has his head in a book. Do you ever get jealous?"

"Not really. When we first married, I sat by his side in the library and assisted him in his various research. It made us even closer. And now that we have a baby, Melvin's research is no longer the most important thing in his life." A satisfied glow came over her fair countenance.

"Then your husband adores your baby?"

Catherine Steffington nodded, her long lashes sweeping downward. "Our precious son is no longer a baby. He'll soon be two. But, yes, Melvin's foolish over our little lad. He's a wonderful husband, too, but I do believe our lad is the center of his universe."

How Dot wished her union with Forrester could be as happy as the Steffingtons', how she hoped she could bear Forrester's son and secure a contentment as satisfying as Catherine Steffington's.

Next Dot moved to Sir Elvin. "You must be very proud of your brother."

"That I am." Sir Elvin snatched another glass of port from Topham's tray as the butler moved toward them. "How does the investigation go?" he asked in a low voice. "Did you learn anything from Maryann?"

"Nothing that will lead us to the murderer. We did learn that Ellie had regretted her recent acquisition of money. We also learned she was supposed to meet with a man that last night. He must have been the killer, but Miss Macintosh's friend had no clue as to his identity."

At that point two well-dressed young ladies came up to them, and Sir Elvin introduced them as his younger sisters. Though their resemblance to their brothers was undeniable, they were in no way masculine, nor were they tall like their brothers. She would guess that they were a good bit younger than her, especially the one named Lizzy, who could not be out of the schoolroom yet. Once more, Dot found herself praising their scholarly brother, and the ladies preened.

Next Dot went to Mrs. James Blankenship, who was so deep in conversation with Dot's father that neither noticed when she walked up. When Mrs. James finally looked up, she broke into a smile. "Oh, my dear Miss Pankhurst, thank you so much for inviting us to your wedding Wednesday. I cannot wait. I'm so happy that you and dear Appleton are marrying."

"Thank you. I'm very happy, too, but I especially want to compliment you on your son. How proud you must be of him. He's terribly clever and was most entertaining."

"Thank you, my dear. I couldn't be prouder." She sighed. "There is only one thing that could make me happier."

Dot quirked a brow.

"He and Mary have been wed almost two years. . ."

Dot understood. "You fear they're unable to conceive children?" Mrs. James nodded. "Don't get me wrong. I love Joy and Baby Gregory dearly, even though they're not of my own flesh."

Dot had almost forgotten that this woman was Blanks' stepmother.

"But what mother doesn't want to see her child carried on?" the woman asked.

"I understand."

"I advise you not to worry about it," Mr. Pankhurst said. "Two years isn't so long. They can still have children."

Mrs. James directed a dreamy smile at Dot's father. "I do hope you're right."

What a night this has been for personal reflections, Dot thought. She could not remember any time when people had spoken so candidly on such personal topics.

"Mrs. James Blankenship has done me the goodness of permitting me to accompany her to the Pump Room tomorrow," Mr. Pankhurst said.

Dot was most pleased, especially since she had plans of her own the following day, plans she had no intentions of sharing with her father. Or anyone, save Forrester and Annie.

Forrester came to her and offered her a glass of port. "I have noticed that you've been so busy being the perfect hostess you've neglected to imbibe yourself."

She thanked him as she took the drink.

He lowered his voice. "A pity they don't make muzzles for young ladies."

"Perhaps you judge Abby too harshly, my dearest." Dot placed a gentle hand on his sleeve. "You must make allowances for her tender age."

"You, my love, are much too tender hearted."

A grave expression on his face, he shook his head. "Would you believe that Annie had a long talk today with our youngest sister to urge her to weigh all of her words before she blurted them out?"

"No, I wouldn't. Perhaps Abby's shortcoming is hearing?"

"My sister hears perfectly."

"Then her problem must lie with comprehension."

"I don't know. I assure you my other sisters are highly intelligent—much like my Dot."

She loved it when he referred to her as *My Dot*. "You must make allowances for her youth."

He shook his head. "The word *punishment* was used by Jonathan Blankenship tonight. Perhaps that's what Abby needs. Were she punished for tonight's thoughtless outbursts, she might learn to think before she speaks."

"I will own the futility of my efforts to train my naughty cats by punishing them when they, for example, attack my newspaper. Punishment has not been successful."

He grimaced. "It would work with dogs."

"You surely wouldn't harm her!"

"Never. I was thinking of not allowing her to attend certain fetes until she can demonstrate the appropriate social graces." His gaze fanned over the assemblage. "Everyone enjoyed tonight's salon very much, and we still have whist to look forward to. Quite a successful night, I'd say."

"Mrs. Moreland was just saying she'd like to have the next salon soon at Winston Hall. "But next time, Abby will not be permitted to attend."

"It sounds too cruel, even if it might be effective."

Annie came to them, and Forrester apprised her of the plan to "punish" Abby.

"I vigorously endorse such a plan," she said. Then she turned to Dot. "Speaking of that wretchedly careless sister of ours, I wanted to tell you I won't be able to join you and Timothy tomorrow. I had promised to go with Abby to the dressmaker's, and it will take most of the day. My sister is the most undecisive person ever to draw breath."

"And what is it we're supposed to be doing tomorrow?" he asked Dot, a mock look of sternness on his face.

"Annie and I were speaking of finding the scene of the murder," Dot whispered.

"And how," he asked, "do you propose to find this?"

"I'll show you tomorrow."

Since all the tables were set up, she encouraged her guests to pair up for the games. It did not escape her attention that her father claimed Mrs. James Blankenship for his partner. She and Forrester were partners against

Catherine and Melvin Steffington. She was amused that Sir Elvin's table included Annie, who was his partner, Agnes, and his eldest sister, Ann. The two youngest sisters, Abby and Lizzy, did not play but sat together on the sofa, giggling and sharing confidences.

This first time she had played whist with her future husband, she discovered they made a good pair, even though the competition from the Steffingtons was stiff.

It was well past two in the morning before her guests left. Forrester was the last to leave, and she suspected it was because he wished to steal a kiss. Which he did in front of the fireplace when everyone else had gone.

"Are you sure you want to look for the place of Ellie's murder tomorrow?" he asked.

Still flushed and feeling weightless from their kiss, she nodded, her eyelids heavy.

He pressed one last kiss to her cheek and left.

Chapter 18

"So you've got some notion that we'll be able to find the spot where Ellie Macintosh was murdered." Appleton's gaze moved from Dot to that damned orange cat with that ridiculous name.

To annoy him even more, the furry creature leapt upon his lap and curled up as if he meant to affix himself permanently. Already, Appleton could see that the pesky feline was shedding a mixture of white and ginger-coloured hair onto his dark brown breeches.

Digby was *not* going to be happy. His valet was far more particular over his master's clothing than Appleton himself was.

From the delighted expression on Dot's face, one might have thought the queen herself was bestowing a royal visit at the Pankhurst residence. "Oh, look how sweet! Lover Boy adores you."

Why couldn't the beast understand when it was neither wanted nor appreciated? A dog would have known. But, then, dogs were intelligent. He could not say the same for cats. Bothersome creatures.

He was at a loss as to how to respond. He could hardly risk telling her how unfavorably he looked upon her cherished cat. Lying was something he'd always avoided. He lifted a stiff hand and attempted to pet the cat.

The animal started to make a deep, rumbling sound but continued to stay coiled on Appleton's lap and look as if he were sleeping. What the devil? He looked up at Dot.

If possible, she looked even more delighted. "You've made Lover Boy's purr practically roar with satisfaction."

So that's what it was! *A purr*. "You mean this is a sound of . . . cat contentment?"

She nodded happily. "Indeed it is. Contentment of the highest order. You may never get Lover Boy to leave your lap."

Not at all what he wished to hear.

When he stopped his stiff-handed petting, the cat's eyes opened, and to Appleton's astonishment, the cat's paw went softly to his hand as if to urge him to pet him some more.

Perhaps Appleton *had* underestimated the beast's intelligence after all.

"He wants you to resume petting him," Dot said.

"I realize that." He reluctantly started stroking the soft pelt.

Appleton was quite certain the beast had concocted a plot to torment him for his lack of affection. Damned animal.

"We are fortunate that it's another sunny day to aid in our quest."

"But are you not forgetting that we are handicapped by several other factors, the first being that we have no idea where the murder was committed?"

"I realize we don't know where it was committed, but we can make hypotheses."

How did a woman know about hypotheses? Scientific method was out of the realm of what was taught to young ladies. As smart as Annie was, he was almost certain she would have no knowledge of that word. "And what is your hypothesis?"

"We are almost certain she was to meet her murderer before she went to work the night of her death. Correct?"

He nodded.

"Wouldn't it be a good assumption that the meeting might have taken place between her lodgings and Mrs. Starr's establishment?"

He had to agree.

"And," she continued, "since we know he dumped her body in the river, would it not make sense that the crime must have been committed near the banks of the river? He could hardly be seen carrying a dead body around the city."

"You do have a valid point."

"But you don't sound convinced."

"Oh, I'm fairly convinced. It's just that nearly two weeks have passed. We had three straight days of unrelenting rain—not to mention that if the murderer realized he might have left something that was potentially incriminating, he's had ample time to retrieve it."

She nodded thoughtfully. "There's merit to what you've pointed out, but I still think we should make every effort to investigate."

"There's one more consideration. The Avon is a very long river." He sighed. "But I suppose we should start somewhere."

"I agree."

Appleton would be most happy to get this animal off his lap. A pity Digby wasn't here to brush the cat hair off his breeches.

As he and Dot walked along the pavement

toward the city center, he mused about their mission. While he gave it little chance for success, he did concede it was a good day for a walk, the warmest yet in a cool autumn.

A scattering of trees throughout the city were shedding their leaves of rust and gold. How sad that Ellie wasn't alive to witness the transformation of summer to winter.

He hoped to God they would be able to identify the person responsible for her death. No one deserved to die more than the despicable fiend who'd murdered her.

But he mustn't dwell on her death. It wouldn't bring her back. His energies would be better directed at finding her killer. "How, my dear Dot, do you propose to walk along the River Avon when much of its frontage is across people's private property?

"I can't think of everything. I'm relying on you to determine how we're to examine as much riverside as possible. You're the man. And a lord, too. Who can deny you?" He chuckled—though he had to reluctantly admit there was some truth to what she said. People were always intimidated by titles of nobility. It had been his experience that oftentimes he met with inordinate success merely by mentioning his title. "You would agree, would you not, that she had to have gone into the water north of the Pulteney Bridge?"

"Undoubtedly."

"Then I suggest we just start walking along the river, on its west side, of course."

She nodded.

That's what they did as soon as they reached the distinctive bridge. The area near where the river bank and the Pulteney Bridge converged was highly populated. "This could not possibly be the scene of the murder," she said.

"I agree. He would have to have selected a more remote location for his dirty deed." It was the dirtiest deed that could possibly be committed.

During the next half hour's walk, the riverbank was surrounded by fairly dense population, most of which looked to be private houses. At any moment he expected someone to shout at them for infringing on property, but to his surprise, they didn't see a single soul.

He was telling Dot about the dogs he kept at Hawthorne Manor—in answer to her questions—when he saw something that caused him to pause. *That is where the murder occurred.*

He eyed an ancient church—more of a chapel, really. Could Sunday service still be held there? The old church's stones had become black with age, and it was so small, he doubted more than two dozen worshippers would be able to gather within its walls.

Who would be here on a weekday night? He felt almost certain the murderer would have asked Ellie to meet him here under the cover of darkness.

Then he would have murdered her. No one would have been around to see him lug her body and toss it into the nearby river.

Dot clutched his forearm. "That's got to be it!"

"I was thinking the same thing."

"They can't still be worshipping here," she said as they came closer to the old church. "The place looks as if it hasn't been used in years."

"More like centuries."

When they reached it, he tried the weathered

timber door, not expecting it to be unlocked. It opened, its hinges groaning from disuse. They both stood inside the musty vestibule for a moment as their vision adjusted to the darkness, and then they strolled into the tiny church.

Dot ran a gloved hand over the back of the last pew. It left a patch of thick dust on her pale blue glove. Not a single hymnal or Book of Common Prayer was in evidence.

"Your suspicions are right. The church is no longer used for religious purposes," he said. It sickened him to think of what this former house of worship might be the scene of nowadays.

She walked to the nave and stood there for a moment, her face as solemn as a hired mourner's. "She was murdered here."

"You can't know that."

"I feel it."

"Then I suggest we invoke the scientific method, and . . ."

"Look for clues." She began to walk toward the miniscule sanctuary. There was no longer an altar at the front of the church. With each step, she looked left and right, paying particular attention to the rough stone floors covered in dirt.

He moved behind her, duplicating her actions and looking in the same places she had already looked. When they reached the sanctuary, she went to the right, he to the left.

Almost indiscernible in the church's dim light, especially in the dark corner, a scrap of red fabric was gathering dust. His stomach sank. Ellie often wore a red dress when working at Mrs. Starr's.

He moved to the corner as if he were approaching a poisonous viper and bent to pick it up. The red was still vibrant, proving it had not been there for long. It was a moment before he could trust his voice. "Did the newspapers say what Miss Macintosh was wearing when they pulled her body from the river?"

He had not been able to read the accounts. Having known the victim, it was too disturbing for him to see her tragic death sensationalized, to know that every person in Bath had access to every morbid detail of her murder.

Dot whirled toward him. "You've found something!"

His voice was as grim as he felt when he said, "Perhaps."

She raced to the other side of the church. "The newspapers said she was wearing a red dress."

His breath hitched.

When she saw what he held, her eyes shut tightly. "This is one time when being right brings no satisfaction."

He put an arm around her and drew her close. "I know. It's wretched."

He hated being here, knowing this was where poor Ellie had been lured to her death, knowing this was where she had drawn her last breath.

He didn't like Dot being here. For the first time since he and she had begun their inquiries, it occurred to him he was putting Dot's life in jeopardy. What if the killer learned that they might be able to identify him? The murderer would hasten to permanently silence them.

And the monster had already proven adept at overpowering the fairer sex.

All Appleton could think of was getting Dot out of there. "We need to go."

"We most certainly are *not* leaving yet. If we found something to indicate Miss Macintosh was here, we might just as easily find something that may point us to her killer."

That *was* the reason they had come. He hated to acknowledge that he'd gotten so alarmed at finding the location of Ellie's death that he'd forgotten what their initial quest had been. "A pity the light in here is so poor."

"But you've already had great success—as sad as it may be." She looked up hopefully at him. "I pray we can be as fortunate in locating something that belonged to the killer."

He looked down at the torn piece of red fabric. "This proves there was a struggle."

She nodded somberly. "If she were fighting for her life, it stands to reason she might tear off something of his."

He agreed.

"What size was Miss Macintosh? Was she tall, per chance?"

"No. She was average size. Neither small, nor tall."

"So if the killer were taller than average—as that old woman described the man in Sydney Gardens with Ellie—she would have been overpowered fairly quickly. Unfortunately."

He nodded solemnly. Not finding anything else in that same corner, Appleton moved toward the very back of the sanctuary and began to walk the perimeter. This was the darkest part of the church. He went slowly and stooped over. It was difficult to clearly see the dull stone floors because they were covered with dust and dirt and droppings from assorted creatures he dared not mention to Dot.

He found nothing of interest along the entire interior perimeter of the church and began to move toward its center. Something shiny and small caught his eye. He bent and picked it up and examined it. He knew at once what it was and where it came from.

A smile swept across his face. "Success!"

She raced to him. "What did you find?"

"Something that can possibly lead us to the killer." He opened his palm to reveal a shiny brass button.

"A button?"

He nodded. "Not just *any* button. This is a button exclusive to coats fashioned by the London tailor Redmayne."

She frowned. "I was hoping it would be the killer's monogram."

"I will own, this isn't as good as a monogram, but it does tell us the killer has to be a wealthy man because Redmayne is one of the most expensive haberdashers in the Capital."

"So it's a safe assumption that the killer is likely a man who knew Miss Macintosh from Mrs. Starr's?"

"It would be a sound guess." Appleton placed the button in his pocket. "Come, love, let's get out of here." He wanted to get Dot into the sunlight and away from this grisly place which even smelled of decay. "We can discuss this on the way home."

Neither of them spoke until they were well clear of the old church and far from the River Avon. It was as if they were trying to purge themselves of the stench of death associated with the rotting old church.

"How do you know about the buttons? You've used Redmayne before?"

"I have."

"What of your friends?"

He shrugged. "Most of my friends use Bath tailors. I'm one of the few who spends time in London because my father—then my brother—served in Parliament and always kept a house there."

"What about the other patrons of Mrs. Starr's?"

"That's a different story. Many, many of them have ties to London. Many of them don't live here year round as my friends do. As you know, Bath society is mostly transient."

"But how many of the men at Mrs. Starr's use Redmayne?"

"I'd never before given it any thought."

"And now you've pledged not to go there anymore."

"I never go back on a pledge." His voice was stern. "But Sir Elvin can always be my eyes and ears there, just as he set up our meeting with Ellie's friend, Maryann."

"Just as I felt sure Ellie Macintosh was murdered in the old church, I feel we're getting closer to learning the identity of her killer."

He took no comfort in her words. Being at the site of Ellie's murder made her death even more harrowing.

Now he worried about Dot. And Annie. He wished he'd never allowed them to participate in this madness of trying to apprehend a killer.

Chapter 19

"I'm going to London in the morning." Forrester made the statement as they were walking up Broad Street, using the same toneless delivery as if he were stating a well-accepted truth, like "My eyes have always been green."

He need not explain. She knew he intended to visit the establishment of the tailor Redmayne. Selfishly, she did not like to think of him leaving Bath, did not like the thought of not being able to see him.

Yet she realized his trip could yield the identity of Ellie Macintosh's killer. "You're going to the tailors?"

"Yes."

"Do you anticipate being able to make the trip in one day?"

He chuckled. "You have little understanding of English travel if you think that possible. Leaving at dawn tomorrow I'll have to ride like the wind to make London by nightfall."

She pouted. "Then you'll be gone for two whole days or even longer?"

"You sound disappointed," he said playfully.

"I am. I shall miss you."

He lifted her hand and pressed his lips to it. "I shall miss you, too." He paused, his step slowing. "Will you promise me one thing?"

"Of course."

"Please do not go *anywhere* without someone—a man—to guard you."

She was taken aback—taken aback and flattered—over his genuine concern. Ever since they had left the scene of poor Ellie Macintosh's death, she had sensed that something oppressive was weighing on Forrester. Now she realized he was worried about her. "I give you my word," she said.

* * *

A costly coach was parked in front of Appleton's house. The black paint of the carriage shone as if it had just left the carriage maker's. Not even a speck of dust marred its perfection. Its coachman sported scarlet livery, a jaunty top hat resting on his aging head, lending an aristocratic air to the equipage. But to Appleton's dismay, no crest distinguished the conveyance.

"Who could be paying us a call?" he said to Dot.

"Then that carriage does not belong to one of your friends?"

"Not unless one of them has recently procured a new coach. A very expensive one."

They entered the house, and voices, along with his sisters' tinkling laughter, came from the upstairs drawing room. He and Dot hurried up the staircase, but when he drew close to the drawing room, he recognized Henry Wolf's voice and went as rigid and cold as a steel cutlass.

She sensed his tenseness and shot him a quizzing glance. "What's wrong?"

"That man, Henry Wolf, has dared to call upon my sister."

"I'm sure he means no harm."

"You. Don't. Know. Him." Appleton stormed into

the chamber. All three of his sisters, their pretty gowns fanned out upon the silken chairs and sofa where they sat, looked most agreeably upon the obnoxious man who had the audacity to seat himself on the same sofa as Annie.

Appleton felt like striking Wolf. Or challenging him to a duel.

Annie looked up. "Oh, here's my brother and his fiancée."

Wolf's face clouded. He stood, as would any gentleman upon a lady's entrance into the chamber, and he observed Dot with eyes that were narrowed to slits.

Wolf was the last person Appleton wished to know about his forthcoming marriage. He'd not wanted the man to learn that his marriage to an heiress would enable him to claim the IOUs before Wolf could claim his property—or try to claim Annie.

Wolf spoke icily. "I did not know you were getting married."

"Yes," Appleton said. He refused to elaborate.

"They're to marry next Wednesday," Abby interjected.

Anger surged through Appleton. Why could Abby never keep her mouth closed? Wolf was so devious, he might try to find a way of stopping the wedding from taking place.

Why was Henry Wolf so obsessed with Annie? Just purchasing the IOUs from Mrs. Starr would have cost a king's ransom. Yet he was willing to hand them back to Appleton and not even seek a dowry. All in an effort to make Annie his wife.

Which would never happen as long as Appleton drew breath.

Appleton wasn't the only angry man in the

chamber. Wolf could barely conceal his fury as his gaze shifted from Appleton to Dot. He quickly feigned civility. "I regret that I must leave as soon as you've come, my lord, but I have exceedingly enjoyed my stay with your delightful sisters." His gaze went to Annie, and he bid her good-bye.

Appleton ignored him, directing his comment to Annie. "I thought you would still be at the dressmaker's."

A puzzled look on her face as she eyed Wolf's back while he left the chamber, she said, "We just returned as Mr. Wolf drove up. He wasn't here more than a quarter of an hour."

Appleton glared at Annie and did not speak until the house's front door closed. "Have I not warned you against that man?"

His sister bristled. "Honestly, Timothy, I am three-and-twenty years of age—old enough not to have to have my brother screen my callers."

"I have never screened your callers. Wolf is the only man I've ever tried to shield you from."

"Well, I found him to be a perfect gentleman," she said, jutting out her chin with an air of defiance. "And you cannot deny he's sinfully wealthy."

"You must trust me on the depravity of the man's character."

She glared at him and stalked from the chamber.

He turned to the other sisters. "Neither of you will encourage that man's attentions in any way. Is that understood?"

Her eyes wide, Agnes nodded.

His angry glance moved to Abby. She shrugged. "I did not find Mr. Wolf appealing in the least. Even if he is possessed of a great fortune."

His sisters left the chamber.

"I'll see you home in the coach," he said to Dot, "and then I'll be early to bed for I have to leave before dawn."

* * *

Appleton lost count of how many times he had to change horses on his journey to London. He'd denied himself for so many hours, his hunger had abated, only to be replaced with a gnawing void in the pit of his stomach. He would not permit anything to keep him from making Redmayne's establishment before it closed this day.

Night came early this time of the year. When he finally reached Savile Row in London, lanterns lighted the shop's doorways against the darkness, and each shop window was illuminated from within.

Through the large window at Mr. Redmayne's premises, a well-dressed man was hanging up a jacket. *Thank God, I'm not too late.*

Appleton handed off his horse to an hostler and entered the shop.

"Ah, Lord Appleton," a smiling Redmayne said, "how good it is to see you." The tailor's discerning eye swept over his patron's dust-covered boots and the general disarray of Appleton's clothing. "Have you come from Bath?" As a good businessman, Redmayne was obliged to be acquainted with the habits of the men who patronized him.

"Indeed I have."

The tailor's brows lowered. "I will own, my lord, I'm surprised to see you since it was only last month that you took possession of three of those coats which I am gratified to say you admired so much."

"What a good memory you possess. As it happens, I've come for information. It may be a matter of life or death. I can say no more." *Death.* Ever since he'd visited the place where Ellie was murdered, he feared another death was imminent.

Even worse, he feared for Dot's safety.

"Pray, my lord, what information could I possibly possess that could be so important?"

"Has anyone purchased a replacement of one of your special buttons in the past two weeks?"

Redmayne's eyes widened. "As it happens, I did receive such an order—and I was instructed to send it to an address in Bath!"

Appleton's pulse thundered. His stomach went queasy—and not from hunger. He was about to learn the identity of Ellie's killer. It was likely someone he knew. All day he'd been hoping Redmayne could provide this information, and now that he was going to, Appleton felt sick. "His name?"

"Humphrey Mitchell."

Appleton internally slumped. It couldn't be Mitchell! Appleton had known him all his life. In fact, the man was the father of Abby's closest friend. In all the years Appleton had been gaming at Mrs. Starr's establishment, not once had he seen the affable family man there.

Appleton would stake his life on Mitchell's innocence. But not Dot's life.

He looked at Redmayne, who was an inch or two shorter. "Anyone else?"

The tailor shook his head. "Not recently."

Appleton clasped a hand to his shoulder. "Since you are possessed of so fine a memory, I should be interested in knowing which other men with ties to Bath are clients of yours."

"Besides yourself and Mr. Mitchell?"

"Yes."

Redmayne stroked his prominent chin. "Your Master of Ceremonies at the assemblies, Mr. James King. He's a loyal patron of my business. And one of my wealthiest clients had a new jacket sent to Bath recently. He's a very good customer. As you must know, my lord, my services don't come cheap. All of my clients are either of the nobility or very fine gentlemen."

"Who would that wealthy client be?"

"Oh, that would be Mr. Henry Wolf."

Appleton felt as if he'd plunged from the top of Westminster Cathedral. That queasiness he'd been experiencing expanded. He not only felt sick in his gut, his heart ached. He was almost certain Wolf was the murderer.

The realization brought no comfort.

He looked into Redmayne's eyes, which reflected the glow from a nearby oil lamp. "You've been exceedingly helpful."

As Appleton swept from the shop, Redmayne called after him. "Will you tell me why this is a matter of life or death?"

"Once everything's sorted."

He went straight to Appleton House in Mayfair, where a skeleton staff of two looked after their London home. They looked surprised to see him.

"I'm just here for one night," he told the male servant who answered the door. Appleton did not know his name. "I won't require a proper dinner, but please send something—I don't care what—up to my chamber. I've not eaten all day. Then I'll be off to bed, for I must rise before dawn—which I did this morning."

With each step up the staircase, his worry

mounted. He could not dispel the fear that Dot's life was in peril.

He could not forget the look of sheer hatred that briefly distorted Wolf's face when he eyed Dot the previous day after learning she was to marry Appleton.

* * *

Her father's coach drew up in front of the Blankenship residence on Queen Square. "Now, Papa," Dot said, "have a care about not getting in your cups in front of Mrs. James Blankenship. You want to make a good impression."

This would be the first time her father and the widow with whom he was so enchanted would be together socially.

"That's good advice, my pet. I *do* want to make a good impression. The lady mentioned she did not approve of her late husband's excessive affinity for strong spirits."

"There you have it—another good reason not to indulge."

Her father collected the lady, and they rode on to the theatre. "Lord Appleton has done us the goodness of permitting us to use their family's box tonight," Mr. Pankhurst told his companion as they entered the opulently decorated lobby and moved to the staircase.

Dot hoped the widow did not find her father's frequent references to *Lord* Appleton tedious. Dot herself refrained from doing so. After all, she would soon be Lady Appleton, and she fervently hoped the mere addition of title did not alter her in any way. Unlike her father, she was not rendered foolish in the presence of nobility.

She did understand that after nine-and-forty years of living, this was the first time her Papa had been on intimate terms with a peer, and such a connection elevated his own self-worth.

Still analyzing her father's behavior as they took their seats on the front row of Forrester's box, it suddenly occurred to her that her father's ailments as well as his dependence upon spirits might have been misinterpreted these past few years.

What if his physical limitations were borne from the need to have someone make a cake of themselves over him? It had been two decades since a woman—other than his silly daughter who coddled cats—had shown him love. The need for love between a man and woman was as elemental as the need to draw breath. At least, that's what Dot now believed, now that she'd fallen in love with Forrester.

Even her father's craving for brandy and port could merely be filling his loneliness. Dot felt guilty she had not been more understanding. Their relationship was closer than that of most fathers and daughters, but now that Forrester had come into her life, she understood there were different kinds of love, and her father's love for his daughter was no replacement for loving a woman and being loved by a woman.

Even as the play—Sheridan's *School for Scandal*—started, her father and Mrs. Blankenship showed more interest in each other than in the actors upon the stage. It did not escape Dot's notice when her father drew Mrs. Blankenship's hand into his own. And he did not release it throughout the entire first act.

Although Dot was exceedingly happy for her father, his intimacy with Mrs. Blankenship made her miss Forrester even more.

At intermission, a liveried young man entered their box. "Is Miss Dorothea Pankhurst here?" he asked.

"I am."

He handed her a note and left.

She unfolded it. It was from Forrester's best friend, Sir Elvin.

My Dear Miss Pankhurst,

I am concerned about Lord Appleton. Please meet me in the lobby.

Sir Elvin

Her heartbeat exploded. She'd been uneasy about Forrester's journey. What if highwaymen robbed him—or worse?

Her father and his lady love were so deep in their own conversation, they scarcely noticed she was in the same box. It took her standing and clearing her throat to capture their attention. "I'm running down to the lobby. I'll be right back."

As soon as she reached the bottom of the stairs she scanned over those assembled. With his height, Sir Elvin should tower above most of the assemblage. But she did not see him. She moved into the throng of unfamiliar male faces. Then she saw the chalky face of Henry Wolf.

He smiled. "Are you looking for Sir Elvin?"

"Yes."

"He awaits you outside. Here, allow me to show you where he is."

Her first thought was that Sir Elvin must not have the same aversion to this man as Forrester did.

Two or three very fine equipages with liveried drivers sitting upon the box lined up in front of the theatre. Was Sir Elvin in one of them? Why would he be expecting her to come to him? Was it not more gallant for him to have come to her?

"He's just around the corner," Mr. Wolf said.

When she saw that the side street was not illuminated as the one in front of the theatre, she became nervous. Forrester's words came back to her as resonant as if he were standing beside her. *Promise me one thing. Please do not leave your house without someone—a man—to guard you.*

And here she was, leaving the theatre without her father's protection. And at night.

An uneasy feeling creeping over her, she turned to go back to the well-lighted street, but Wolf clasped her arm so hard she winced in pain. He yanked her close and with his other hand held a sizable knife to her throat. "Make a sound and I'll kill you."

Chapter 20

With the knife's point pricking her throat, her attacker forced her to a waiting phaeton and demanded that she climb up onto it. He stayed next to her as if they were stitched together, his forearm hooked around her neck. She was afraid if she moved too quickly, the knife would slice into her.

Most peculiarly, once she managed to sit on the perch, he ordered her to take up the reins and drive eastward. This maneuver, she realized, was necessitated by his need to use his own hands to hold the knife below her chin.

Horrifying thoughts cascaded over her. This evil man had chosen to come in a phaeton instead of his magnificent carriage because he wanted no witnesses, not even his own servants. Nausea rose up as if she'd ingested hemlock.

She now knew, without a doubt, this was the killer of Ellie Macintosh. He—not Sir Elvin—had written the note to lure her from the theatre. He must know of the close connection between Forrester and Sir Elvin.

But why did he want her dead?

Fear paralyzed her vocal chords. Was he one of those maniacs who took pleasure with women—then even more pleasure by snuffing the life from them?

As soon as she realized he was directing her toward the river, she was certain he was going to return to that decayed chapel where he'd murdered his last victim. The ribbons vibrated from the trembling in her hands.

"Why are you doing this to me?" she managed, her voice choked by tears. "You don't even know me. What have I ever done to you?"

"I don't hate you. I hate your Lord Appleton."

Her head snapped in his direction. Moonlight diffusing through the cloudy night made his colourless face seem even more macabre. A chill spiked down her spine. "Everyone admires Lord Appleton. How could you possibly dislike him?"

"You're right. Your Lord Appleton has always led a charmed life. He's everybody's friend. Except mine. He took great pleasure in competing against me—and always rubbing my nose in my inferiority. Fencing. Riding. Even mathematics. Did you know he and his friends had an unflattering name they called me—behind my back?"

"He never mentioned any such thing in my presence."

"They referred to me as The Penguin," he snapped viciously.

"Then why is your argument with him and not with his friends?"

"I loathe Appleton more. He didn't think I was good enough to even introduce to his precious sister. He gave me the cut direct at Almack's."

"But why do you hate me?"

"Because I wish to deprive Appleton of your fortune. I want to see him grovel before me. I want him to beg me for money, beg for me to give him back the deed to his house."

Her fortune? Did everyone in Bath know she was her father's heiress? How she wished she had been born a pauper. "You know not Lord Appleton if you think him capable of groveling in front of anyone."

She was on a precipice between life and death. He would undoubtedly murder her. Would he slit her throat?

How could she get away from this man? These streets to which he was directing her were as dark and empty as Bath before dawn. A pity no one could help her.

What did she have to lose? When she approached the next intersection and he instructed her to turn left, she slowed the phaeton. Then she leapt onto the street, but she lost her balance on landing and fell, her knee grinding into the cobbles. Oblivious to the pain, she sprang up and started running. Even though she tried to run faster than she ever had in her life, she resembled a cripple hobbling from a burning building.

The thud of his leap from the vehicle followed, and as fast as she tried to run, he was gaining on her. She must run to the public house she knew to be two streets over. She had to go where there were other people.

Blood pounded in her head. Her lungs felt as if they would explode from the exertion. Her legs felt as if she were plowing through mud. And her knee throbbed with every uneven step. As hard as she tried, she couldn't outrun the killer who was on her heels.

Then she saw the light illuminating the tavern's sign some hundred yards ahead. Her salvation.

Faster and faster she ran. Now the Crow and

Anchor was only fifty yards away, then twenty, and then the vile man raced up from behind and knocked her to the street.

* * *

Appleton had left his London house before dawn. He wanted to be in Bath before dark. He wouldn't have a moment's peace until he saw for himself that Dot was safe. He'd tortured himself worrying about her.

He was convinced that Henry Wolf was responsible for Ellie's death, and he was reasonably certain that he now knew why. It sickened him to realize that indirectly he had contributed to Ellie Macintosh's murder. Now all the pieces of information had merged into a complete narrative.

Because of his hatred for Appleton, Henry Wolf wanted to ruin him. He must have paid Ellie handsomely to drug Appleton and see to it that he not only lost his ability to reason but also all his worldly riches.

Wolf also wanted Annie, lovely Annie from an aristocratic family, to be his bride. That sickened Appleton almost as much as worrying about Dot.

Then, to complete his fiendish plan, Wolf had to kill Ellie because she was the only one who could reveal the depths he'd sunk to in order to ruin Appleton. Wolf wouldn't be able to count on her continuing to conceal their cheating scheme. Rightfully so. She'd already regretted her actions. Had she, perhaps, threatened to disclose his scheme to ruin Appleton?

During the long, grueling journey back to Bath, Appleton pondered Wolf's meeting with his sisters. Could Annie's tongue have slipped, allowing Wolf to know that her brother and Dot were investigating Ellie's murder? One little slip to the vile man would have been enough to put Dot's very life in jeopardy.

And I'm not there to protect her. He vowed that when he returned to Bath he would march her to the church and marry her. As soon as he revealed to the magistrates the identity of Ellie's killer.

He hoped to God his worry was all in vain. He hoped that when he arrived at their house, Dot and her father would be enjoying a quiet game of chess.

At no time in his thirty years had he ever felt more certain of impending danger than he had since he'd left Dot. Dear, sweet, loving Dot.

It shamed him now to recall how ambivalent he'd been to all her fine attributes when he'd first met her. Now that they'd grown close, he'd come to love everything about her.

That ridiculous affinity of hers for cats he now found endearing. It was only one facet of her loving nature. She had demonstrated how well she would fit into his family. She and Annie were already like sisters. She was also a fine daughter, and she would be an excellent wife.

His chest expanded when he thought of her becoming a mother, a mother to his children. She would be a wonderful mother. He swallowed hard, his very heart aching for this to come to pass.

Please, God, allow her to be safe.

When he had offered for her, he had not then known how fortunate he would be to have her for his wife. Why did it have to take this separation, this paralyzing worry, for him to realize how very dear she had become to him? Now he knew that he could have looked the length of England, from the moors of Yorkshire to the white cliffs of Dover, and he could not have found a finer woman than Dot to wed.

He would have been bored to death with a wife who lacked intelligence. He would never have to treat Dot as one would a dimwit.

The longer he knew her, the lovelier she had become. Her dark beauty stood out from all the insipidly fair maidens in the same way a swan stands out from a flock of mallards.

He longed to pull the pins from her luxurious mane of mahogany hair and comb his fingers through it. He never tired of looking into her near-black eyes. He yearned to draw the smooth curves of her luscious body against him and kiss her senseless.

Yet with every pound of his horse's hooves, he agonized that he'd never see her again.

I'll kill Henry Wolf.

* * *

He raced straight to her house. The butler informed him that the Pankhursts had gone to the theatre. Even though Appleton was covered with dust and most definitely *not* dressed for the Theatre Royal, he hurried there. He then fairly flew up the stairs, going straight to the Appleton box, oblivious to those staring after the ill-dressed interloper.

He froze when he saw her father seated there with Mrs. Blankenship. *But no Dot.* "Where's Dot?" he demanded, panic in his voice.

Mr. Pankhurst turned around, a shocked look on his face when he saw how Appleton was dressed. "I'm not quite sure. She received a note at intermission and left. She said she'd be right back."

"But that was some time ago," Mrs.

Blankenship interjected.

Appleton's heart felt as it would pound out of his chest. "How long?"

Mr. Pankhurst's lips pursed. "Perhaps fifteen minutes. I assume she joined some other young people."

"Did she say who she was meeting?" Appleton asked.

"No."

"Do you know where she was going?"

"To the foyer."

Appleton was sick. He hoped to God he was wrong, but he was terrified she was with Henry Wolf at this very moment. "She's in danger. We must find her."

Mr. Pankhurst leapt from his seat.

"You look for her in the other boxes," Appleton barked. "I'm going back downstairs."

He rushed to a liveried doorman, who was now the sole occupant of the lobby. "Have you seen a young woman. . ." How could he describe Dot? He had no idea what she was wearing. "She has very dark hair, and I suspect she may have left the building at intermission."

"There was one young woman with . . . I don't mean no disrespect. . ."

"With a bounteous bosom?" Appleton supplied, hope welling in him.

The other man grinned. "Yes, sir. That's how I would describe the young lady."

"Was she alone?"

"It's hard to say. She looked as if she was looking for someone and was reluctant to leave the building, but another bloke said something to her, and she did leave." The doorman shrugged. "I got the impression the two were not together."

"Did he follow her?"

The doorman nodded.

"Can you describe the man?"

"All I remember is his skin was uncommonly white."

Appleton could have fallen to knees and wept like a woman. But he could not give in to his grief. He had to find Dot.

Before it was too late.

Chapter 21

As Appleton was mounting his horse, Mr. Pankhurst came running from the theatre, Mrs. Blankenship struggling to keep up with him. "What's going on? Why is my daughter in danger?"

"I'm afraid she's with the killer."

"Oh, my God!" her father cried out in an anguished voice.

Mrs. Blankenship shrieked.

"I must go," Appleton barked. "There's a chance he's taken her to an abandoned church this side of the river."

"I know it," Mrs. Blankenship said, rushing off to summon the Pankhurst coach.

Appleton couldn't wait. He sped off. He tore through the dark, quiet streets of Bath, and when he reached the Pulteney Bridge, he turned north and spurred on his mount. If Wolf were planning to abduct Dot, he would have had a vehicle that could accommodate at least two persons. Therefore, it would take him longer than a solo rider on a horse to get to the church—if, indeed, that was his destination.

As Appleton neared the church, his blood froze. For just outside the door, a phaeton drawn by a single horse had been tied to a tree.

Please, God, don't let me be too late.

He leapt from his horse and raced toward the

church's weathered door, flinging it open. It was as dark as the inside of a coffin. "So help me, Wolf, I'm going to kill you!" he yelled into the blackness as he rushed from the vestibule into the church.

"Dot! Dot, are you unharmed?"

"Be careful, Forrester! He's got a knife!"

Those were the sweetest words he'd ever heard. He rushed down the nave faintly illuminated from a lantern Wolf had apparently provided for himself. Dot was in one corner, and Wolf stood just before the sacristy, staring at Appleton. Dot had obviously not easily given in to the murderer.

"Get out of here, Dot!" Appleton called. Better that Wolf kill him than his innocent fiancée. Though Appleton rarely carried a weapon of any sort, because he had been traveling today, he had armed himself with a knife. As he stood at the back of the church, he unsheathed it, determined to make Wolf come to him.

Dot scurried around the church's perimeter until she reached him. But she was making no effort to leave. "Go on," he urged her.

She sniffed. Several times. "I can't leave you." Sniff. Sniff. "I couldn't live without you."

"Nor could I without you."

She burst into tears.

Wolf crept down the nave like a tiger on soft paws.

"Please, Dot, for me. You must leave." If Wolf killed him, he'd turn immediately on Dot.

She inched toward the door, and Appleton almost went limp from relief. But he must be on his guard.

Though nothing in his life had prepared Appleton for hand-to-hand knife fighting, he would stay there and face this vile murderer. When they were lads he'd always had the advantage.

With each step closer the murderer came, the faster Appleton's heart beat. He tried to stay in the darkness that shrouded the rear wall. If he moved toward Wolf, the lantern's light would make him an easier target.

Though Wolf wasn't a large man, as he stealthily moved toward Appleton, he seemed far bulker than ever Appleton remembered him. So many thoughts flashed through Appleton's brain. What if the wealthy man's purse had procured for him skilled teachers in the art of pugilism? Or had a superior fencing master instructed him how to swiftly deflect his opponent and go in for the kill?

When no more than a dozen feet separated them, Appleton eyed Wolf's stomach and hurled his knife at the wide target.

Wolf yelped in pain as he sank to the floor, but he still managed to bring his arm over his head to pitch his knife at Appleton.

Appleton ducked. Steel collided with stone. Thank God Dot was no longer standing behind him.

The thundering sound of horse hooves sounded, quickly followed by the church's door slamming open. "Thank God you're unharmed," Mr. Pankhurst said to his daughter. Dot must have stayed in the vestibule.

Still watching the man on the floor, Appleton shifted his gaze enough to see Pankhurst's coachman. His legs planted, the coachman aimed a musket at Wolf.

Dot rushed to Appleton. He crushed her into his arms. "I've been mad with worry," he said huskily as he pressed kisses to her cherished face. "Tomorrow we marry, my much-treasured love."

Epilogue

The wedding had been performed and all the breakfast guests had departed—save one: Mrs. James Blankenship. Forrester came up behind Dot, enclosing her in his arms as he nuzzled his face into the hollow of her neck and traced a path of butterfly kisses. "If we're to reach Hawthorne Manor by dark, Lady Appleton, we must be leaving."

That was the first time she'd been addressed by her new title, and it made her feel as if she'd just imbibed an entire bottle of champagne. And when he touched her like this, she could hardly think of anything except her physical pleasure and how thoroughly she was in love with this man.

"I need to thank Mrs. Blankenship before we go," she said.

That lady, dressed in an elegant pale blue gown, came up to the newlyweds. "You've no need to thank me."

"But thanks to your efforts, everyone who matters to us attended our wedding," Dot said. "Did you even get a moment's sleep last night?"

Mr. Pankhurst had come to stand beside the widow. "Who could sleep? Even had we not been up half the night with the magistrates who arrested that wicked monster, I would never have been able to purge from my mind the fact he almost killed my daughter." He eyed Forrester. "I owe everything I possess to you, my lord." His eyes grew moist. "I can't tell you how much it means to me that my only child will be as cherished by you as she has always been by me."

"Thank you, sir, for entrusting her to me. There's not a happier man in the kingdom than I am today."

"I just might be," Mr. Pankhurst said, giving the widow an amused glance as he slipped his arm around her. "Mrs. Blankenship—Helen—has done me the goodness to consent to wed me."

Dot flung herself at her father. "Oh, Papa! That is, indeed, wonderful news. Now I shan't worry about leaving you." Then she turned to Helen Blankenship. "I am so happy for both of you."

"I shall be very happy to become a member of the Pankhurst family. With each invitation I wrote out throughout the night, I kept thinking how you're to now be my daughter, and I was doing what any mother of the bride would be doing."

"I am very grateful," Dot said. "You certainly contributed to this being the happiest day of my life."

An impatient look on his face, Forrester looked heavenward. "Now that it's settled we are the happiest four persons in all of England, will you oblige me, my dearest bride, by leaving now?"

Dot looked up at him. "There's just one more matter."

"Uh oh," he said.

"Instead of my kitties coming to Hawthorne Manor in the luggage carriage, can they ride with us?"

He gave her a stern look. For a few seconds. Then he broke into a smile. "You've caught me in a charitable mood. After all, it was one of your d---, er, darling cats who brought us together." He leaned into her and brushed her lips with his. "And besides, I am powerless to ever refuse you anything, my beloved vixen."

They finally said their farewells and got into her husband's coach. He pulled her close. No words were necessary. Two hours of marriage could hardly make them feel as one, but that is precisely how she felt at that moment.

She'd never felt more loved. She knew he hadn't been in love with her when he asked her to marry him. Even over the next several days after she accepted his offer and they spent time together, he was not in love with her. But during those days he *had* grown to love her. Her dreams were just fulfilled quite a bit sooner than she had expected.

There was so much she admired about him, but she thought his complete honesty with her was perhaps what she treasured the most. Last night, after the injured Henry Wolf had been arrested, Forrester told her the whole story about how Ellie had cheated to strip him of his fortune. He confessed that he had initially only been interested in Dot's dowry, but that the longer he was with her, the fonder he became of her.

He admitted that at the second assembly he finally began to desire her in the way a man desires a woman. Then after they had visited the decayed church, the worry he felt toward her was so paralyzing he knew it would destroy him if anything happened to her.

And just before he had kissed her goodnight, he'd revealed how tortured he'd been all the way back from London, worrying he would lose her.

"Forrester?"

The pad of his thumb wove circles on her hand. "Yes, love?"

"Have I told you how madly I love you?"

He pursed his lips. "I don't believe you have."

She drew even closer, settling her hand on his thigh. "I do."

An amused expression on his face, he playfully asked, "Do what?"

"I love you. I have loved you almost from the moment we met."

He yanked her into his arms for a most passionate kiss.

Which was interrupted when Lover Boy leapt across the carriage and dug his claws into the back of Forrester's jacket.

"I do believe Lover Boy is jealous of your attentions to me," she murmured.

"Wretched cat."

But he did not permit the animal to deprive him holding his wife in his arms for another exceedingly tender kiss.

The End

Author's Biography

Cheryl Bolen is the *New York Times* and *USA Today* best-selling author of more than three dozen romances. She's also an Amazon All Star author. She's written for Harlequin Historical, Kensington Books, Montlake, and Love Inspired Historical, and has published independently through her Harper & Appleton imprint. Many of her books have placed in contests, including the Daphne du Maurier (romantic suspense) and have been translated into nine languages. She was Notable New Author in 1999. In 2006 she won the Holt Medallion, Best Historical, and in 2012 she won Best Historical in the International Digital Awards, a competition in which she's had five other titles become finalists in Best Historical categories. Her 2011 Christmas novella was named Best Novella in the Romance Through the Ages contest.

A former journalist and teacher, Bolen adores reading about dead Englishwomen. She is married to the retired professor who captured her teenage heart when they were undergraduates. Their favorite pastimes include watching college sports and traveling, especially to England—often accompanied by their grown sons.

She invites readers to www.CherylBolen.com, or her blog, www.cherylsregencyramblings.wordpress.co or Facebook at https://www.facebook.com/pages/Cheryl-Bolen-Books/146842652076424. Super fans can join her Facebook readers' group, Lady Cheryl's Ladies of the Ton at www.facebook.com/groups/817160475466386/.

Made in the USA
Las Vegas, NV
25 April 2024